DRY DOCK

An Epic Realistic Adventure

A Novel by
Mickey Roman

Arise Publishing
www.arisepublishing.com

Copyright © 2013 - Arise Publishing, Inc

All rights reserved. No portion of this book may be reproduced by any process including printing and digital copying means without written permission of the publisher. Brief quotations embodied in critical article or reviews are permitted with proper reference. For information write info@arisepublishing.com

Arise Publishing, Inc
Po Box 19816
Jacksonville, FL 32245

2nd Edition

ISBN-13: 978-1484818992
ISBN-10: 1484818997

Other Titles by Arise Publishing can be purchased at:
http://www.amazon.com/author/arisepublishing

40 Traditional Bed-Time Stories for Children *with Illustration*
30 Days of Traditional Bed-Time Children Stories *with Illustrations*
12 National Bed-Time Stories for Children *with Illustrations*
The Coloring Book, A companion to Traditional Stories for Children Stories

Coming Soon:
The River May - The Story of Jean Ribault
Spanish Moss

Special thanks to:
Cavelle Roman for Graphics, Formatting and Publishing
Wid Bastian with Joy Publishing for Editing
Bob Averill and Jason Delaney for their Technical Editing

One

"Why do I have to go? Africa isn't my favorite place on the planet. Tell me what's going on Keith."

"Mark, I'm not meeting her in town. I've booked a car. We're getting together at her father's ranch or plantation, or whatever they call it. It's thirty miles north of Cape Town."

"You want to drive thirty miles north of the city to meet a girl? You heard the Captain; we are restricted to the ship. I thought that ..."

"This is Olivia, Mark. *Olivia?* The hottest girl on the planet?"

"I thought you said Robin was the hottest girl on the planet, or was it Amy, or maybe ..."

"Mark, I've set it all up for you. Olivia sent me an e-mail with a picture of the guest house. She is having food brought in, a full spread. Videos, a computer - you can call home and Skype with Joy and the kids all night long. What sounds better, the ship's rack or a luxury suite?"

"While I'm chillin' out, you'll be..."

"She could be the one, Mark. She's a hot South African like your wife, trained to submit and please a man... all joking aside, I really...."

Mark Schaefer smiled and raised his palm indicating "enough".

"We get caught and there will be blood to pay. Everlast doesn't take kindly to people sneaking off his ship, especially since our turnaround time is so short."

"Is the gasoline off *The Star*?" Keith asked.

"Yea, we transferred it to the terminal. Still don't understand why we are delivering gas to a port where there's a refinery, but it's done," Mark answered.

"So you're off duty?"

"Yes, so are you. We are supposed to be relaxing on board, not traipsing around Africa."

"The raft is already waiting astern. Nice little boat, big ..."

"Olivia?" Mark asked, already knowing the answer.

"She set it up. The girl is loaded. She has beauty, brains and money. Mark, I mean I'm seriously thinking that..."

"I should have my head examined. Why I let you talk me into this crazy stuff... alright. But we are back here by first light. No exceptions, Keith. First light."

"First light."

The Florida Star, a two hundred and thirty meter long, seventy five thousand DWT Aframax class tanker, was anchored outside of the oil terminal at Table Bay Harbor. It was a beautiful May evening; the sea was dead calm with barely a hint of breeze. After Keith went below to call Olivia and collect his things, Mark walked out on to the deck for a breath of fresh air and to watch the sun set into Port of the Cape of Good Hope.

Mark had been away from home for almost a month now, and it would likely be another six weeks before he returned to Jacksonville. *The Star*'s next trip was headed to Iraq on its standard run to pick up six hundred thousand barrels of crude oil and transport it to the *Louisiana Offshore Oil Port.*

It was easy to calculate how long it took to travel by sea from the Persian Gulf to New Orleans. Mark wasn't concerned about hurricanes and serious storms because in May and June weather was normally not yet an issue. Sometimes an unexpected circumstance or storm would arise on their return leg forcing a brief delay, but for the most part it was a simple matter of mathematics – so much distance covered at a certain speed and then they arrived at their destination.

Seventeen years ago it was different. Mark was young and full of love, while Joy had "miles and miles of legs". They met at a Church event and instantly became friends. His time away kept them from establishing a set routine, but when Mark was in town they had plenty of money, energy and a growing love. Although Joy was from another country, Mark's family and friends accepted her because they trusted him. Years after they met, Mark and Joy were still newlyweds.

Back then the idea that he had to be at sea for eight months out of the year was something they could both live with given the fact that he was paid a top wage as a merchant marine. Mark loved the ocean. The sea was in his blood. Like his father before him, Mark Schaefer learned a trade and applied it to a job aboard ship. Sal Schaefer had been a mechanic and career merchant mariner, a specialist in diesel engines. Sal's son Mark became an electrician, with a strong background in mechanics.

Mark, Joy and their two children were tired of him being a part time father. No matter how hard he tried, things were different now. Where once constant traveling and life on the high seas calmed him down, now he found more solace when he was home. Mark gave his family all he had and then some when he was in port, but there was no way to make up for his absence at the Pop Warner football games, the school plays and for just not being around to comfort his children after they had a rough day at school, or discipline if they did not obey their mother or teachers.

A devout Christian, Mark also knew that there was more to life than money. He believed that he was called to support his family, but support was more than economic. Trouble was, he and Joy had put on "golden handcuffs" - they needed his income to support their lifestyle. There were college educations to be funded along with a mortgage and the rest of the family bills. Mark felt trapped, but he also had faith. God would show him the path; he just had to be faithful and patient.

"Are you going dressed in your filthy overalls?" Keith asked sarcastically, as he reappeared on deck. "I know that I'm the one entertaining a lady, but you could at least hop in the shower and put on a clean shirt and an ironed pair of pants."

Mark smiled and said, "Alright Ace, I'm comin'."

It didn't take them long to pull the launch onshore and find the rented Range Rover parked on Strand Street just east of the Waterfront. Keith and Mark tossed their duffel bags in the back seat and Keith fired up the ten year old SUV. As Mark climbed in, he pulled his silver colored revolver out of his pants and stowed it in the glove box.

"You won't need that," Keith said, as he watched Mark put the gun away.

"It's my *American Express* pistol. I never leave home without it," Mark retorted. "They just left the Rover sitting here with the keys in it?"

"I doubt they're that trusting. We're being watched," Keith said, half jokingly, pointing to a car that was sitting with its headlights off fifty yards away.

"Better than Hertz."

"Even comes with its own GPS." Keith turned on the GPS device. It outlined the route on a road map to Olivia's house and gave an estimated travel time of forty minutes.

"Nice. Keep your speed down. I don't want to have any conversations with the local authorities."

"Take a nap old man. I'll get us there safely."

Keith drove the Range Rover through town, turning north on the N1 Highway. He noticed that they were not being followed. Within a short while the road turned from blacktop to hard dirt. The lights of Cape Town were behind them now, the evening was pitch black. There was no traffic on the bumpy road that was full of potholes.

Mark pulled his cap over his eyes and laid back in the seat. But he was too wired to sleep. "Tell me about Olivia," Mark asked, both from curiosity and from the need to know just what he had gotten himself into.

"Thought we'd been over this ground."

"Tell me again."

"Last run we stopped in Durban. You know, we all had week long furloughs. I stayed in the South

Durban Towers, next to ..."

"Complete waste of money," Mark opined, interrupting.

"Well, be that as it may, Mr. Frugal. There is an art gallery on the first floor of the hotel. I walked in, bored out of my mind, and there she was standing right there in all her glory. I thought for sure she was a movie star or something. Olivia has the body of Halle Berry and the face of Angelina Jolie. Light skin, straight hair, she was dressed to the nines ..."

"So you just walked right over to her and said, "Hi, I'm Keith, a mate on an oiler. Marry me."

"What does Joy see in you exactly? You have no charm, no style and no game. Someday you'll have to tell me about the miracle of your courtship."

"Okay, Stud. Impress me."

"I approached her subtly, not like a bull elephant in heat. I asked her about the painting she was looking at; I listened and 'bounced back' her conversation."

"You made her feel like she was the most interesting person in the room."

"I made her feel like her every thought was the most important thing in the world to me."

"I gotta hand it to ya, Keith. You could charm the

habit off of a nun."

"Two days later we were eating breakfast in bed. That was after a night of ..."

"Save the details, lover boy. I get it. How old is Olivia?"

"She just turned twenty three."

"The fact that you're twelve years older than her, that doesn't ..."

"Olivia is a college graduate. She studied Art History in South Africa and has traveled two times to the U.S.A."

"She is still young enough to be daddy's little girl, Keith."

"She told me that her father was the richest man in their province. He owns thousands of hectares of land, cattle, horses, light industry, he ..."

"Does he know that a thirty five year old American sailor is doing his daughter?"

"Ah..." Keith hesitated. "Olivia says that she is going to tell him."

"Going to tell him?" Mark sat up and pulled his cap back on top of his head. "Keith, assure me that he at least knows who you are and approves of you seeing his daughter."

"All good things in time."

"Are you kidding me right now? What the ..."

"Relax, Mark. Olivia's father is in Uganda on business. The guest house is miles from the main residence. I'm not completely stupid."

"Yes, you are. Completely stupid, I mean. When it comes to women."

"Love you too, my brother."

"Why do I let you talk me into doing these things?"

"You're my Guardian Angel."

"Keith, all kidding aside, please ..."

"Relax, Mark. I've got it handled. You'll have a peaceful night and I'll get to see my girl. You worry too much."

Two

"Wow, she is as advertised," Mark said, as Keith pulled the Range Rover onto the cement driveway of the guest house. Olivia was standing on the lawn waving to them as they arrived. "She is an incredibly beautiful woman, and wait till you get to know her."

"The drive couldn't have gone more smoothly," Keith bragged. "Perfect directions, decent road, no cops or check points. And that while South Africa is going through this Apartheid. Are we happy now?"

"Feed me and we'll see," Mark said with a smile.

The guest house was a complete residence, obviously built as a mini-compound on Olivia's father's sprawling ranch. Nearby the lights of other buildings twinkled in the warm, tropical night. A herd of sheep was making noise in the distance. A few men, well-armed, were patrolling the grounds and there always was a few bushmen with machetes.

"Baby," Keith said, as he embraced Olivia. They shared a deep, passionate kiss.

"My love," Olivia said, cooing.

"This is my best friend, Mark. Mark, Olivia DeJong."

"A pleasure, Olivia," Mark said, removing his hat.

"An honor, Mark. Keith talks about you constantly. I'd say you were more of a big brother than a friend."

"Someone has to look after him," Mark joked.

"Indeed," Olivia answered.

Arm in arm Olivia and Keith walked into the house with Mark trailing a short distance behind. It was decorated in simple elegance. A butler greeted them and asked if they wanted a meal.

Mark jokingly asked, "How about steak and lobster?"

The butler drolly replied, "How do you like your steak prepared and would you like some burnt butter with your lobster, sir?"

Olivia showed Mark where he would be spending the next few hours. The front room had been all set up for him. A laptop was on a small table with a set of instructions for accessing the outside world. A sixty inch plasma TV sat across from the couch along with a selection of DVDs. Several newspapers were stacked on the coffee table.

"Mark, is the room to your liking?" Olivia asked.

"Incredible. Thank you for your generosity, Olivia. This is a real treat."

"I am in your debt. I couldn't bare to go another three months without seeing my love. If you need anything, dial 111 on the phone. The butler will see to your needs," Olivia explained.

"Olivia and I will be in the back of the house. We might go for a swim, who knows. If there is an emergency, please ..."

"I get it Ace, no worries."

"Say hi to Joy for me."

"Will do."

Mark sat down on the couch, put his feet up on the ottoman and looked at his watch. In three hours, if he had the time difference correctly calculated, Joy and the kids would be home. Until then all he had to do was eat his steak and lobster, watch TV and kick back.

The butler brought Mark his food; the steak was perfect, but the lobster was frozen. The butler apologized and offered to bring Mark some fresh jumbo shrimp twenty to the pound prepared with American "Old Bay" seasoning, but Mark smiled and said no. The steak was more than sufficient.

He could not hear Olivia and Keith in the back of the house. Thank God for that, Mark told himself. He put a movie in the DVD player, turned down the lights and settled in for a few hours of peace. Just in case he dozed off, he set his watch alarm for the time when he could Skype his family.

Mark's meal and the relaxed atmosphere did their job. Soon he was napping.

He awoke to the sound of several vehicles pulling up outside in a hurry. Men were shouting and car doors were slamming. Instinctively, Mark searched through his duffel bag, but it wasn't there. He had forgotten to transfer his gun to his bag. As a group of men entered the house he said a silent prayer hoping that his carelessness would not cost him his life.

"Get up, grab your sack and come outside. Now!" the armed man shouted in a British type accent. Mark did as he was told.

There were three black Suburbans parked in front of the house. At least ten men, those were all Mark could see, were spread out around the grounds. One man was going through the Range Rover. He found Mark's gun and tucked it in his pants.

From the side of the house Keith and Olivia emerged, both dressed only in beach towels. Their heads were wet and their feet were bare – obviously they had been swimming.

"What is the meaning of this?" Olivia shouted. "Do you know who my father is? You men will be ..."

As Olivia was yelling, the back door of one of the Suburbans opened. Out stepped an older, well-dressed man who Olivia immediately recognized.

"Daddy!" Olivia shouted, as she ran to her father's side. "Thank God!"

"Oh heck," Mark muttered. He looked over at Keith. All Keith could do was raise his palms upward indicating that he was as surprised as Olivia was.

Olivia's father removed his suit jacket and placed it over his daughter's shoulders.

"Daddy, why are you here? What is the ..."

"Do not speak to me. You have the nerve to sneak around and carry on with this man behind my back? Did you think that I would not be told that you were here with him?"

"Mr. DeJong, please let me explain. It's not what you might ..."

Keith stopped talking when two of Mr. DeJong's men cocked their weapons and pointed them at his head.

Mark muttered to himself, "Please God, tell Keith to keep his mouth shut."

"I love Keith, Daddy. I was going to tell you all about him when you returned from Uganda."

"You do not know this man, Olivia."

"And you do?" Olivia asked.

"Enough of this. Who are these men?" Mr. DeJong bellowed.

DeJong's men took Mark and Keith's duffel bags and dumped their contents on to the lawn. They found what they were looking for very quickly, copies of their passports.

"Americans," the guard said, handing the documents to Mr. DeJong. "Big problem if they disappear."

"Do not hurt them, Daddy. I love Keith. Mark, the other man, was just helping his friend."

Now two other guards cocked their guns and aimed them at Mark's head.

"If you hurt them I will never speak to you again," Olivia warned.

"You will do as you are told, Olivia. I am still deciding their fate."

"Look, sir," Mark said, knowing that he was risking death just for speaking. "Our ship is anchored in port. Our Captain knows where we are. If we do not return at the scheduled time he will call the embassy."

One of the guards then thrust the butt of his AK-47 into Mark's gut.

"Keep your mouth shut," the guard ordered.

"You hit me again and I swear I'll ..." Mark said, as he slowly stood up, recovering from the blow.

As the guard raised his weapon to fire, Mr. DeJong shouted, "Enough! Leave him alone."

The guard backed away.

"I guess it's your lucky day, sport," Mark said, looking the guard straight in the eye.

Three of the guards then huddled around Mr. DeJong. Keith took the opportunity during the brief respite to slip on his jeans and shirt, retrieving them from the pile of his things lying on the lawn.

A minute later Mr. DeJong dismissed his guards and said, "If either of you men ever show your face on my property again, you will be shot on sight. Mr. Keith, stay away from my daughter. She will not be having relations with some lowlife seaman from a tanker. I warn you only once. Never let me hear your name spoken again."

Mr. DeJong got back in his Suburban and closed the door.

Olivia was wrapped in a blanket and escorted into the house. As she was being led inside she kept calling out Keith's name, begging him not to abandon her.

Mark looked at Keith. He did not have to say a single word to convey his message, which was simple – shut up, pick up your stuff, get in the Range Rover and let's get the heck out of here.

Three

A few miles passed before Mark and Keith could be certain that they weren't being followed. The lightly traveled narrow two lane road that carved its way through the countryside made it almost impossible for a tail not to be spotted. Mark was driving because Keith had been drinking steadily since they arrived at the guest house.

Seeing no one behind them, they relaxed a little.

"Mark, I...I had no idea, I mean ..."

"You realize that we could easily be dead. DeJong wasn't playing around, he was all business. Keith, my God! You almost made Joy a widow. Doesn't that ..."

Mark stopped talking because Keith was leaning out the window puking on the side of the Rover.

This wasn't the first time Mark and Keith had narrowly escaped retribution at the hands of an angry man, although in the past the perpetrator had always been a jealous husband or a jilted boyfriend.

Most people thought Keith Toms was a likable rascal, a "big little kid", in Joy's words. No one really took Keith too seriously, except for the women who fell for him and the men he incensed when he stole their sweetheart's affections. But Mark knew that Keith had qualities that were far more worthy hidden behind his charming, "affectionate scamp" persona.

If Keith had a dime, he was apt to give ten cents to someone in need. Sure, he spent money at times on fancy clothes, four star restaurants and overpriced hotels like the proverbial "drunken sailor", but more often than not the reason why Keith Toms lived hand to mouth was simply because he gave his money away.

Whether it was his sister in Omaha with four kids and another on the way or his aging mother in Dallas or just a kid from the street who looked desperate, Keith would open his wallet to them. If any of his friends needed a hand with anything, from moving furniture to fixing a broken down car to baby sitting on a Saturday night, Keith stepped up. He never bragged about his generosity or took any credit for it.

Keith thought Mark Schaefer walked on water. All Mark had to do was ask and no matter what it was Keith would do it for him. Friends like that were very rare, and Mark knew it and appreciated it. But why Keith's "heart of gold" pumped blood through the veins of a man who had absolutely no good sense when it came to women was the great unknown.

Mark tried hard to remember all of Keith's good qualities at times like these because otherwise he would probably have just opened the SUV's passenger door and dumped him out on the side of the road.

"You know we can't go back on board yet," Keith reminded Mark.

"Herman," Mark mumbled.

"Yep, he doesn't rotate off of watch until two a.m. Then Evan's up to bat and we're cool. He's expecting us," Keith explained.

"We'll just sit in the Rover until two," Mark pronounced.

"Right where the bad guys could find us, if they had a mind to," Keith offered.

"Ideas?" Mark asked.

"Let's leave the Rover downtown. I'll call my contact and give him the location. Then we cab it to a place a few miles away, hunker down and wait until one thirty or so and take another cab back to the launch."

"There isn't anything open at this hour except for bars," Mark said. "You've had enough alcohol for one night."

"I'll stick to club soda."

"I'll tell you what you will do," Mark said, as they stopped at an intersection. "You will sit down right beside me and mind your manners. No more drama, Keith. I mean it. I just want to go back to *The Star* and get the heck out of here. Understood?"

"Club soda. No problems. Best behavior."

"Fine. Now where am I going?"

Keith had spent a couple of days on leave in Cape Town three years ago so he knew the general layout of the town. They dropped the Rover off on the east side of the city along Voortrekker Ave. Then they took a cab to a bar near the Camps Bay Beach. From the bar it was a five minute trip to the launch.

The Mamba Club was an upscale establishment that catered to tourists and wealthy locals. Typical of Cape Town in general, the opulent nightclub was situated in the middle of rows and rows of shanties. Mark and Keith were definitely not properly dressed for the establishment, but since they were white and American the doorman would almost certainly let them in.

As it turns out the doorman was a doorwoman, so Keith had little trouble gaining admittance.

The music was techno-rock, definitely not Mark's favorite. The club was only about three quarters full, probably normal for a Thursday night. Mark and Keith found an empty table in the back and settled in for three hours' worth of watching Camps Bay "hottest babes" shake their backsides to the thumping sound of mindless beats.

Mark's watch alarm went off. It was time to call Joy. He definitely wasn't going to do that from the club, nor was he going to let Keith out of his sight even for a few minutes. Mark sent his wife a text message, "Keith up to his old tricks. I'm cool, but close call. Have to talk later. Love you, kiss the kids for me." A few seconds later Joy sent a text back saying, "Be careful. Understand about Keith. Love you too."

"I'm so glad that I'm not single," Mark said, an hour into their Club Mamba session. "The only proper word to describe places like these is lame, named after a deadly African snake called the Black Mamba."

"You can't tell me that you don't like looking at gorgeous women. I know you better than that, Mark."

"I'm not dead, just happily married. I miss my wife. This skank display only makes me miss her more."

"See the four ladies across the way?" As Keith said this he smiled and waved to the girls, who smiled and waved back. "They've been staring at us ever since we walked through the door. I think it's you they like, Mark."

"Keith, so help me God, if you ..."

"Have I done anything? I've been sitting right here, until now."

"Whoa, where are you going?" Mark asked.

"To the bathroom, if that's alright with you. Wanna come along and help me out? Lend me a hand?"

"Straight to the head and straight back. I'm in no mood, Keith."

"Yes sir!" Keith shouted as he stood, saluted Mark and left to take care of business.

Because the club was filling up, Mark didn't notice that one of the girls excused herself also. His attention was drawn to the three rough looking men that had now joined the women across the room. Although he was not familiar with the local customs, Mark Schaefer knew scum when he saw it. They spoke the universal language of trouble loud and clear.

"Miss me?" Keith said when he slowly returned.

"What time is it?" Mark asked.

"We have half an hour left to kill."

"Lord have mercy."

"Wanna dance? I'll let you lead."

"Always clowning. Do you take anything seriously?"

"Wise man say, 'Don't sweat the small stuff and everything is small stuff'."

"Have you even given a thought to poor Olivia?"

"Of course I have. I'll call her when we're at sea and clear of this place."

"Don't tell me that you're going to see her again."

"Okay, I won't tell you."

"Keith, why ..."

"You boys have no business in here," the very large, very dark skinned black man said, leaning over Mark and Keith's drinks. He'd ventured over from the table where the ladies had been eyeing Mark and Keith.

"Excuse me?" Keith said.

Keith started to get up, but Mark grabbed his arm and said, "Sit."

Two other rough looking men now joined the belligerent man at Mark and Keith's table. They displayed pistols tucked in their belts.

"You should keep your pet on a leash," the large black man said, gesturing to Keith. "He bothers our women."

"He's done nothing to your lady friends. He's sat right beside me for the past two hours," Mark replied.

"Are you calling me a liar?" The large black man backed up a step and puffed out his chest.

"We'll leave. Now!" Mark said.

Slowly, Mark and Keith stood, grabbed their duffel bags and started to walk away.

"So you are seamen. Figures. And what is that abomination around your neck? A cross? You're

Christian garbage, probably American too."

The large man spat on Mark Schaefer as he walked past him.

Mark stopped. He calmly wiped the spittle off of his cheek and set his bag down. Keith knew what was coming, it was inevitable.

The large man was laughing, and made a comment in another language, believing that he had humiliated his opponent into submission. Mark just smiled and said nothing. Then in a well-practiced and swift move, he shattered the large man's right kneecap with his steel toed boot.

It was on. Keith hit the man nearest to him and the other thug came at Mark. Soon they were flying over tables and exchanging blows. As the large man who was now hobbled rose to join the fight, Mark grabbed his gun, rolled over a table and discharged a round from the weapon into the ceiling.

Calmly, Mark said, "All we want to do is leave. We don't want any trouble."

One of the men reached for his gun.

"Don't do that," Mark said. "I will not hesitate to shoot. This ain't my first rodeo. Both of you drop your guns on the floor and kick them over to me."

The men did as they were instructed. Keith picked up their guns.

"I hope you recover after your surgery," Mark said to the man whose knee he destroyed. "You might want to think twice before you insult a stranger in the future."

"Mark, we need to leave," Keith begged.

As they backed out of the club and hit the street a cab was idling by the curb waiting for a fare. Mark and Keith tossed their duffel bags in the back seat and jumped into the taxi. They told the driver to head to the spot where they left the launch.

"Will this night ever end?" Mark asked.

"That was not my fault. All I did was say hello to the girl outside the bathroom. She approached me; I didn't come on to ..."

"Do you think the launch is still there?"

"Fifty-fifty," Keith replied.

"If it isn't we steal another one or go for a long, cold swim."

The launch was still there, right where they left it several hours before. The old outboard fired right up and soon Mark and Keith were gliding through the smooth black water under the light of a full moon towards the waiting *Florida Star*. Mark dumped the pistols over the side before leading the way up the rear ladder of the ship.

"Mark, I want to tell you ..."

"We're alive and unhurt." Mark interrupted as he grabbed his friend's arm in an Indian style grip, to help pull him over the edge of the last step into the ship. "I always have to bail you out."

Evan pretended not to notice as Mark and Keith walked across the deck and headed to their bunks to catch a couple of hours sleep before *The Star* departed for the Gulf at first light.

Four

At dawn *The Florida Star* got underway and left Table Bay. Mark and Keith both reported to their duty stations promptly at five a.m., although Keith was more present physically than mentally. All was in order in the Engineering Section so Mark had little to do but watch gauges and supervise the standard routines of his men.

After *The Star* cleared port, Mark took a break and went topside. He was pleased to see Cape Town moving farther away as *The Star* churned steadily east and north toward the shipping lanes in the Indian Ocean. He had half expected to be roused in the middle of the night by whoever was on watch and informed that the South African police wanted to arrest him and Keith. Mark said a silent prayer thanking God for protecting him.

The weather was exceptionally mild. The sun burst out when *The Star* cleared the marine layer fog bank, instantly transforming the sea into a dazzling array of sparkling points amidst deep blue. Mark looked at his watch. It was nine a.m. It was time to call Joy. He walked to the aft section of the tanker and found his quiet spot, a chair strategically placed mid-deck between two large pipes. The crew called it "the phone booth" because when cell service was available and the weather was pleasant, it is was the best place to sit in privacy and talk on the phone.

"Hey," Mark said when Joy answered the call.

"Hey yourself. Are you okay?" Joy asked.

"By the grace of God."

"Do I want to know?"

"No. Same story, different players. I'm just happy to hear your voice. I love you very much."

"Mark, please be careful. I love Keith like a brother, but if he ..."

"Let's talk about the kids," Mark said, interrupting.

"Fletcher wants a *Wii*. All of his friends have one. We didn't get him one for Christmas because his grades weren't up to speed, but his report card is a whole lot better now. Can I buy him one?"

"What do you think? Will he spend all day on the thing?"

"Probably. He's twelve, Mark. Fletch plays games with his friends, you know."

"Your call, babe."

"Thanks. Thanks a lot. Make me the bad guy."

"Hey, it's not like that. I just ..."

"Mark, things have to change. I know how much you love me and the kids and we are so proud of you, but you've got to come home. I'll get a job, whatever is required. We need you here."

"Joy, we've talked about this. I thought we ..."

"I love you, Mark. Yea, we've talked about it. Remember what you told me? When I reached done I needed to tell you? I've reached done, honey. You need to come home."

"What's happened?"

"Nothing, babe. We love you and miss you and we just..."

"Joy," Mark said, somewhat sternly.

"How do you always know?"

"Because you're an open book, easy to read, at least for me."

"Jill is pregnant."

"Chrissy's friend?"

"Yea."

"What's that got to do with ..."

"I'm worried about Jeff's influence on Chrissy, and for that matter, Jill's too. I want to trust her but...do I have to spell it out for you?"

Mark didn't say a word for a minute. He was enraged. Not at Jeff or Chrissy, at himself, at the situation. He prayed for strength.

Responding to the silence Joy said, "Honey, try not to be angry. At least our Chrissy is not fooling around. She's angry at me for not trusting her."

"This is my fault. If I were there I could help be the manly and fatherly influence she needs at this critical stage"

"You want me to lie to you, honey?"

"No, I don't. Okay, okay. What are we going to

do, Joy? I can't make eighty grand a year in Jacksonville. All the benefits too. This is not a .."

"Can we pray about it?"

"Of course, sweetheart. Where is Chrissy?"

"At Church with the youth group."

"I need to talk to her right ..."

"Wait a few days, Mark. I've got her on a short leash. Jeff is off limits. Give her some time to think before you pounce on her."

"If I come home we will have to make do with less. Be sure, Joy."

"I'm sure, Mark."

"Then I will get serious as of now. I will start calling people at the Yard."

"Billy really likes you. He would give you a job if one was open."

"The Yard was sold a few months back. Some New York outfit owns it now. I heard rumors that they're going to bust the union and fire everybody. But, yea, I'll call Billy. Maybe ..."

"Schaefer, report to the Captain on the bridge," the voice on the loudspeaker called out.

"I heard that," Joy said.

"Call you later?" Mark asked.

"Can you call back in twelve hours?"

"Yes, of course."

"I love you Mr. Schaefer. I know this will be tough, but the thought of you being in my bed every night makes me very happy."

"Love you too, babe. We'll work it out."

"Schaefer, report to the Captain on the bridge. Immediately," the voice boomed again.

"Gotta go," Mark said and then hung up. He tucked his phone in his pocket and moved quickly towards the bridge.

"Sir," Mark said as he arrived. "Reporting as ordered."

"Mark," Captain Everlast said. "We have a problem in the bilge."

"I was unaware of any problem, sir."

"We have an excessive amount of oil down there, maybe a two inch layer on the surface."

"Any idea of the source of the leak?" Mark asked.

"No! Evan spotted the oil, but not the source. Get on it, please. Last thing we need is a bilge fire."

"Yes sir. May I ..."

"Enlist as many men as you need to do the job."

"Yes sir."

"Oh, and Mark?"

"Yes, sir?"

"The next time you and Keith decide to sneak off my ship without telling me you will no longer be employed on this vessel. Am I clear?"

"One hundred percent, sir."

"Good. We won't speak of the matter again then."

"Yes, thank you sir."

Mark left the bridge with his tail between his legs. Not only were things unsteady at home, now he had disappointed his Captain, and for what? To help Keith nearly get them both killed? He reminded himself that his decisions were his destiny. He vowed to make better choices, to make sure that he always put good sense and his family first.

Second Mate Evan Peterson was in the Engine Room manning his station when Mark found him.

"We have a problem in the bilge?" Mark asked.

"Yes sir," Evan answered. "'Bout an inch or more of oil floatin' on the surface. Just noticed it today. Weren't there last week when I checked."

"Where's it coming from?"

"Don't know, but I suspect one of the fuel lines that's feedin' the generators. Them pipes are older than dirt and corroded."

"As of now you and Herman are on it. You are relieved of your duties here. Check the fuel lines, identify the leak and report back to me. This is top priority."

"Where's Herman?" Evan asked.

"I'll send him your way," Mark answered.

"I'm on it boss."

"Evan, for all of our sakes, be careful. No sparks. If you're down there and that fuel gets ignited, well, it isn't going be pretty."

"Yea, ah...I'll be real careful."

"You do that."

Five

"Okay, I understand Mark. The leak is stopped?" Captain Everlast asked.

"Yea, Evan and I patched the pipe, but I have issued a standing order that the bilge be inspected every twenty four hours. Those pipes should be replaced, sir. Next time the leak might be far more serious."

"Put it on the list. *The Star* needs an overhaul. We are months overdue for dry dock. The company keeps putting it off, Lord knows why."

"Yes sir. We'll monitor the situation closely."

"What's happening with Mr. Toms?"

"Sir?"

"Keith Toms, your traveling companion? He about took Upton's head off last night in the chow hall over next to nothing, or so I was told. Why is he so on edge?"

"Didn't know that he was, sir."

"Speak with him please, Mark. I don't have the patience required to baby-sit and the man listens to you. If I step in, it won't be good."

"I will talk with Keith, sir."

"Good. One more thing."

What now? Mark thought but did not say.

"Yes sir?"

"I put you in for a raise. It was granted. Eight grand more a year. That makes you the top paid Engineering Department Head in the company. Well deserved too. Congratulations."

Mark was stunned. He had no idea that Captain Everlast had put him in for a raise.

"Thank you, sir. I appreciate your vote of confidence in me. Lord knows Joy and I could use the extra pay."

"After this trip, I'll see to it that we dry dock for over a month. The ship needs the work and we could all use some extra shore time."

"Thanks, Captain."

"Good evening, Mark."

"Evening, sir."

Now what? Mark asked himself. He had reached the top rung for a sea position, unless he wanted to pursue a Captain's slot, which he did not. The next promotion would be to a desk at corporate, or more accurately an executive job that would require him to travel as much as he was currently at sea.

Ninety grand a year! Mark's head was spinning with the possibilities. He was considering everything he could do with the extra cash. He could properly feed the kids' college funds, replace their ten year old Chevy, buy Joy that....

Is Chrissy also having sex like her friend Jill? She denies it but how can we be convinced. She's sixteen. If she makes poor choice like that, what other choices could she be considering? Drugs? Dropping out of school? Was she losing her faith? What about Fletcher? What was he thinking about doing?

Was this raise a trap? A temptation? Mark wasn't sure, but he knew that he needed to ask God and let Him decide.

"Keith," Mark called out above the roar of the giant diesel generator. "Take five and come with me."

Keith Toms put down his tools and walked with Mark out of the Generator Room, through a couple of hatches and into a quiet compartment.

"Mark," Keith said. "What's up?"

"I'm here to ask you the same thing."

"I don't follow."

"What happened with Upton?"

"Oh that. He has a filthy mouth, you know. He started making some racist comments, I got mad, we yelled at each other. No big deal, at least I didn't think it was."

"You've been skulking around here since we got back from our little romp in South Africa. Why? I'm not mad at you, if that's what you think."

"It's not that, Mark."

"I'm listening."

"You'll think I'm an irresponsible jerk."

"I already know that you're an irresponsible jerk."

"Megan is pregnant." Keith said with a transparent

got-caught look.

"Who is Megan?"

"Jacksonville Megan? Father owns the Greek restaurant on Main Street Megan?"

"You're telling me that you are the father of this child?"

"So she says."

"How long have you known about this?"

"Megan told me the day after we left South Africa."

"Do you believe her?"

"Maybe, I'm not sure. Probably."

"It's possible then?"

"Yes, it's possible."

"You had to know this day was coming, Keith. We reap what we sow."

"She wants to have the baby. She wants me to marry her."

"Having the baby, of course. If you created a life, you are responsible for that life. As for marriage, Keith, what do you want me to tell you? You're not ready to marry anyone."

"This whole thing is freaking me out. I mean, I've always been careful. But Megan and I, well we just didn't use proper precautions sometimes."

"Sometimes?"

"More than once, yea."

"Time to step up, Keith. How far along is she?"

"Four months."

"Does that fit the time frame that ..."

"It fits."

"Welcome to fatherhood, my brother. There is nothing better in this world."

"Part of me wants to be a dad. I might be good at it, some parts of it, anyway."

"If you need to talk to someone about this, come to me. Stop biting people's heads off around here. The Captain sent me down here to talk with you."

"Oh geez."

"Yea, the last thing you need right now is to lose your job."

"Thanks, Mark. If I can be half the father you are I might be doing alright, huh."

"Sure, Keith. Let's eat dinner together tonight. We gotta get back to work."

After they parted ways Mark did some hard thinking. Was he a good father? A good husband? He was a good provider, he was honest and dedicated.

But he wasn't present, not nearly enough.

If he wasn't home to love on his family, how good of a father could he really be?

Six

Every member of *The Florida Star* crew, from seaman to Captain, had his own cabin furnished with a desk, an easy chair, a reading lamp, a large clothes locker and a wide, soft berth. With books on the desk and family photos on the wall, the cabins could easily be mistaken for oversized college dorm rooms.

When off duty, the crew of *The Star* could watch movies in a theater that seated ten to twelve, play cards or video games in the lounge or check out music or books in the ship's library. Meals were prepared by a professional chef.

A three bed hospital staffed by a trained nurse provided medical care. He also assisted as a safety officer. Floors in the living areas were covered in rubber tile to reduce the strain of standing and walking on steel decks.

While not the most modern or newest tanker, *The Star* was a very pleasant place to live and work.

Newburg Shipping had put off needed maintenance for *The Star* for nearly two years. The company had been hit with a rash of small and not so small problems with other tankers in its fleet, so the company kept postponing scheduled retrofits in order to fulfill its transport contracts. While *The Star* was barely twelve years old, its required five year overhaul was now twenty one months overdue.

During the trip from South Africa to the Gulf, Mark and Evan repaired two more small leaks in the pipes that supplied diesel fuel to *The Star*'s two electrical generators. Every trip to the bilge was now a hunt for leaking diesel.

When he wasn't on duty, Mark Schaefer now

spent most of his time in his cabin writing down his options and mulling over his future. He liked to spell things out on legal pads. He put the "pros" on the right and the "cons" on the left and then went back and forth between them carefully weighing each aspect of his decision.

After four or five late night debates with himself Mark knew that he simply had to find a job on land. He also discovered that he loved the sea a whole lot more than he had ever admitted to himself or to Joy. As a youngster he became a seaman almost by default, following in his father's footsteps. Truth be told, he had never seriously considered any other career. Why he wasn't sure, it was just the way his life unfolded.

Mark had become accustomed to the solitude, the peace of life at sea. He knew that he would miss waking up, grabbing a cup of coffee and standing on deck watching the sun rise over the water. The smell of the ocean mixed with the odors from the ship was something he was used to and it gave him comfort. He wanted to be with Joy and his children every moment he was away from them, but he had to be honest with himself and admit that he also enjoyed the almost half of his life that he lived alone.

Simply quitting was not an option, he would have to find new employment before he left Newburg. His first thought was to try and go to work at St. John's Shipyard, as Joy suggested. The General Manager of the yard, Billy Caesar, had been a close friend for years. A day or so after sending Billy an email inquiring about employment, he got the response he feared that he would.

Since the acquisition of the Yard by Bowman Industries several months earlier everything had changed. For decades St. John's was a family run business. Andy Larken inherited the Yard from his father in 1955 and ran it until his death a year earlier. Unfortunately, there was no heir to step into Andy's shoes and carry on the family legacy. Andy's two children had moved away from Jacksonville long ago and neither wanted to do anything with the shipyard other than to sell it and cash out.

Andy Larken had tried to find a local buyer for the Yard for years, but met with no success. St. John's was a big operation requiring large amounts of working capital. Profit margins were steady, but not robust. St. John's had a very unique culture – everyone who worked there was treated like family. The safety record of the Yard was unparalleled. The men who worked at St. John's enjoyed what amounted to lifetime employment.

From an investment point of view St. John's Shipyard was troublesome. Buyers were afraid that the culture Andy Larken created could not be sustained after his passing. Profit margins were low because the Yard was not run with profit as its only goal, or even its main goal. In order to bring the margins up, the culture would have to change. Labor costs would have to be reduced as would operational expenses.

Andy held on as long as he could, but a day after his ninetieth birthday his heart stopped beating. He was only in the ground for a month or so when his oldest son Chad announced that the Yard had been sold to Bowman Industries in New York. No doubt, Chad Larken had been negotiating a deal with Bowman well before his father went to his final reward.

As Mark read in his email from Billy, the old Yard was now a memory. Some yahoo named Jabber Campo had been brought down by Bowman from New York to run the Yard. He was a "complete jerk", according to Billy, who "only wants to fire everyone, bust the union and destroy this place".

While he would start sending out discrete feelers immediately, Mark was convinced that finding a top paying marine job in Jacksonville would not be easy. He knew that he would have to take a pay cut. As with everything in his life Mark did all he could do, prayed and tried to have faith that God would lead him down the path He wanted him to follow.

It took five days for *The Florida Star* to reach the Iraqi Offshore Terminal near Basra, Iraq. Loading and unloading of oil are always the busiest times on ship. As the Engineering Officer, Mark had to sign off on the transfer plan and closely monitor machinery and men as *The Star* went about the tricky business of taking on 600,000 barrels of crude oil.

Once *The Star* was moored, communications were established with the Iraqi terminal. A series of protocols were followed, connections made and then pumping began. Loading started at a slow pace and then increased to a steady flow to be sure that all the connections were secure and the equipment was working properly. The steady pressure was held until the "topping off" phase was reached. At that point the crew of *The Star* opened and closed valves to direct the flow of the product and finally signaled the terminal telling them to stop the flow. The Captain ensured proper trim for the ship by adjusting water ballast as the oil was pumped into the empty tanks.

After several hours moored at the terminal, *The Star* was headed back out to sea eastward through the Persian Gulf, out of the Straits of Hormuz and back to the Indian Ocean.

In 1990, when Saddam Hussein was desperately trying to protect his regime from a looming American invasion, the Iraqi Navy heavily mined the waters near where the Iraqi Offshore Oil Terminal now sits. Countless sweeps by American and other naval forces were thought to have removed every mine from the area many years ago.

Somehow an Iraqi contact mine that was originally moored beneath the surface broke free and drifted into debris. It was pulled down thirty feet below the surface in a violent storm. The remnants of the mine's mooring chain then became entangled in an old wreck. The mine sat harmlessly and undetected amidst the twisted metal on the bottom for over twenty years.

Until today.

The old chain finally corroded and the mine broke free. It drifted to the surface and floated out toward the shipping lanes with its fifteen hundred pound explosive charge still very much alive.

Seven

"Thought you'd be up here," Mark said, after finding Keith standing near the bow of the ship scanning the ocean ahead of them with his powerful binoculars.

"Hey Mark. Wanna take a peek?" Keith asked.

"Sure." Mark liked surveying the ocean too, particularly near port.

"I've thought a lot about what you said to me," Keith said, as he stretched and leaned back away from the rail. "I need to step up. It's time."

"Do you remember how we met?" Mark asked, not taking his eyes off the water.

"How could I forget? Still got the scar?"

"You know it," Mark said, almost bragging as he handed the binoculars back to Keith. "Trevor's braces are forever imprinted on the first knuckle of my right hand."

"I was an idiot."

"Yea, you were, but Trevor was being a jerk. He should have backed down when you got the bunk assignment. He knew better, but he didn't give a rip."

"You knocked him out cold. Right then and there I knew it was a mistake to mess with Mark Schaefer."

"I ain't that tough. Just stubborn, I guess. Never could stomach ignorant fools. As I've gotten older hopefully I've become mellower and perhaps even more tolerant."

"There's a pirate in South Africa with a blown out knee who might disagree with you."

"Have you talked with Megan?"

"Just got off the phone with her."

"And?"

"She was in tears, as usual, still says that the

baby is mine. She swears that she hasn't been with anyone else since our first date ten months ago."

"What does your gut tell you?"

"I need to be sure, Mark."

"That's called prudence. It's a virtue. But Megan will need proper pre-natal care and support before you can take a paternity test."

"She has decent insurance, so that's covered. It will help a lot for me just get home and see her. As for the whole marriage thing, I...well..."

"You're not ready for that, Keith. My opinion only."

I ag...what on earth is that?" Keith said, reacting to something he spotted floating in the water.

"Dolphins? Whale?" Mark asked.

"No, it can't be. Has to be some floating debris that looks like...can't be."

"Let me see. Where am I looking?" Mark asked.

Keith pointed to a spot on the water about a thousand yards away and ten degrees to port.

"What the heck! Like you said, can't be," Mark said after a few seconds of looking at the object.

"What if it is?" Keith asked.

"It's drifting right into our path. We will hit it. My

God in heaven..."

Mark stopped talking and started running as fast as he could towards the bridge. He didn't have any way of signaling the bridge because the bow squawk box was down. All he could do was wave his arms around like a madman, as he ran towards the mid ship squawk box.

Jude Upton and Captain Everlast watched in concern as Mark ran full speed towards the mid ship communication phone.

"Schaefer, what in the ..."

"Captain," Mark said, trying to catch his breath as he burst into the Control Room. "Less than ten degrees to port, nine hundred yards away. What is that floating in the water?"

Captain Everlast used the powerful scope on the bridge and quickly spotted the object. Then he barked the following order, "Left full rudder, Mr. Upton. Increase speed. All hands to emergency stations. This is not a drill."

A violent alarm blared over the ship's loudspeakers and the crew sprang to life. Mark and Keith, who had now also reached the bridge, were unsure where to go and what to do.

"Captain, I take it that ..."

"It's a naval contact mine, Mr. Schaefer. I've seen enough in my day. What on earth it's doing out here...Get the navy on the line!" Everlast shouted. "They have some ships in the area on a training exercise. If we hit that thing... explosives don't mix well with crude oil."

"You're turning into the mine," Mark said.

"Yes, if we're lucky the current will push it past us. Turning this floating skyscraper isn't easy. We need some help from the drift."

Everlast hesitated then said, "Schaefer, Toms. Get everyone off of the bow. In fact move everyone above and below decks as far aft as they can go, except for essential personnel. If we hit it, it will be on the bow, I think."

"Yes sir," Mark said, as he started to run again. "Keith, go below. Check as many sections as you can for stragglers, verify and lock down the bulk head doors in case we flood, but regardless get out of there in three minutes." Mark's order was interrupted by the Captain announcing the evacuation of all forward sections. "I'll sweep the deck; make sure no one is left up front."

Mark ran forward, looking from side to side as he

did, hoping to catch anyone that might have missed the call to evacuate. Seeing no one he headed to the bow, Keith's binoculars in hand.

Unable to help himself, Mark stood on the bow of the massive tanker. The mine, and it was very clearly a floating naval contact mine, was barely four hundred yards ahead, directly in the ship's path. *The Star* was headed north, away from the mine. The mine was headed south, drifting with the current.

"Need a little help here Lord," Mark prayed aloud. "Push that thing out of the way, please. Thanks."

Mark took a deep breath and started to run back to the bridge. By his best estimate, he might have time to reach the bridge before they hit the mine. Barely.

The mine might not be functional, Mark thought as he churned his legs as fast as they would go. It's probably very old, maybe it's inert.

But then again perhaps not.

Mark made a mental note of the location of the lifeboats. As he did so he heard choppers and looked up. The U.S. Navy had reached the scene. At least they would be around to rescue the crew assuming that *The Star* didn't ignite like a Molotov cocktail when it hit the mine.

Out of breath and panicked, Mark reached the bridge.

"Feed that video link in here," the Captain ordered. "For once maybe some of this internet and hi tech stuff will actually help us."

One of the Navy helicopters had a video camera tracking the mine. The monitor on the bridge sprang to life displaying the Navy's video feed.

"My God," Captain Everlast exclaimed. "This is gonna be close."

As *The Star* was angling away, the mine seemed to slow its southward drift and moved back toward the tanker. With less than a hundred yards of separation the mine appeared to be unavoidable.

"All hands! Brace for impact!" the Captain shouted into the mike.

Mark's gut tightened. Where was Keith? Mark wondered. Why wasn't he on the bridge?

The video operator on the helicopter now zoomed in on the mine. It looked to Mark like something straight out of World War II, a big grey sphere with foot long projections that no doubt triggered the device when they came in contact with metal. Now the separation was less than two hundred feet. *The Star* was angling away, and the angle was suddenly increasing. A pick up in the current was pushing the mine out of the ship's path.

Mark watched as Captain Everlast grabbed hold of his chair anticipating an explosion. He held his chair so tightly that his knuckles turned pale white. Then, just as it was about to clip the bow of *The Star*, the mine was gently brushed away by the displacement of water as the hull moved forward at high speed. The mine bobbed and floated away from the ship. Two minutes later and the danger was behind *The Star*. The Navy helicopters then circled above the mine and began the process of neutralizing it.

"Where have you been?" Mark asked as Keith reappeared.

"Don't ask," Keith answered. "Are we safe?"

"Yes," Captain Everlast answered. "Mr. Schaefer asked you a question, Mr. Toms. You were told to report back here immediately. Why the delay?"

"Herman," Keith anwered.

"Mr. Openia? What in the world was ..."

"He was asleep with headphones on. No one roused him. When I didn't see him on deck, I went back down after him."

"Those were not your orders, Mr. Toms," Captain

Everlast said.

"No sir, but I figured if we hit it, we might have a minute to run topside before, you know. If Herman was trapped down there and couldn't get out, well..."

"Dumb thing was probably a dud anyway," Mark said, trying to deflect the Captain's attention away from Keith.

As if on cue, a loud explosion and a huge water spout erupted beneath the helicopters. Instinctively everyone cringed and ducked, but it only took a second to realize what had happened, the mine exploded.

"A dud huh," Captain Everlast said, doing his best to maintain his composure.

Keith looked at Mark. They were both thinking the same thing. Where would they be right now if Keith hadn't chosen that moment to stand on the prow and look at the water? What if they had just said, "Nah, it couldn't be" and waited only a minute longer to alert the Captain? What if...

"I guess you bailed us out this time, Keith," Mark said.

"My God, Mark. I mean we coulda been blown to Kingdom come."

"God was looking out for us."

Eight

"How many times have you been around the Cape of Good Hope, Mark?" Keith asked. "Over fifty. I stopped counting after that," Mark answered. "I've also been around Cape Horn, South America twelve times. I got my sea wings when I was twenty one."

"Almost twenty years at sea?" Evan Peterson asked, after taking a sip of his coffee.

"Nearly," Mark replied.

"What's the plan?" Keith asked. He, Mark and Evan were finishing an early breakfast.

"Captain said we are stopping at Lagos. Another tanker, the Iron Lady, is minus a NAV computer. We've got a spare, so we need to deliver and install it. We'll probably take on some fuel as well," Mark explained.

"Never been to Lagos," Keith observed.

"And you won't be going ashore this trip either, Keith. Already asked, we are restricted to the ship," Mark added.

"Aye aye, sir," Keith said, laughing.

"The Captain knows about our South African adventure," Mark said, wiping the last remnants of toast from his face.

"So does everyone else," Evan added.

"I wonder how he found out." Keith asked, looking straight at Evan.

"Hey, don't be given me the evil eye! Herman saw you guys ditch the launch and climb back on board. That dude gets up at least twice a night to smoke a cigarette," Evan said.

"It doesn't matter, Ace," Mark said. "Cap let it go. After the mine incident, you're back in his good graces. Stay that way."

"I finally got to talk with Olivia," Keith said.

"Who is Olivia?" Evan asked.

"She is the reason we went ashore in South Africa," Mark said.

"Olivia is 'restricted' to her apartment in Cape Town. Her father took her passport. I ended it, Mark. Olivia is absolutely the most stunning creature I've ever been with, but I have other priorities now. She needs to get on with her life too."

"How'd she take the bad news?"

"Not well. She cried and we talked, but eventually it became awkward so I just hung up. She has tried my cell several times since, but I can't call her back. I have to let her go."

"Wise move," Mark complimented.

"How 'bout I give her a try?" Evan asked.

"Dream on, Evan. She's outta your league," Keith said.

"How do you know? I might ..."

"Calm down, lover boy. Olivia is outta my league too," Mark said, laughing.

The galley window provided a good view from The Starboard side of The Star. Keith was watching the Cape of Good Hope shoreline pass by in the distance as the ship moved westward.

"It's beautiful," Keith observed. "I can see why you never get tired of the life, Mark."

"This may be my last trip boys," Mark said, getting up to refill his juice glass.

"What did you say?" Keith asked, not believing his ears.

"I may not make another run. I have to find a job on land."

"Joy is mad at you? Is she sick? Is she..."

"None of that, Keith. I need to be home with my kids. They come first."

"Gotta job yet?" Evan asked.

"No. Might take a while too. I just...I'm thinkin' out loud I guess. You boys keep your mouths shut; I don't need to start the rumor mill churning."

"Mark, my God. I just can't imagine going to sea without you on board. All these changes..."

"Keith my boy, I'm not dying. You'll be fine when I go. I shouldn't have said anything."

They sat around the table sharing stories and relaxing until the time came for Mark and Keith to start their watch. Evan headed off to bed.

Mark was really feeling it now, the very strong

possibility that he may never serve aboard *The Star*, or any other vessel, ever again. This made him sad, but the thought of curling up in bed with Joy every night was wonderful. He reminded himself that none of this was about him anyway; a job was only a means to an end. His identity came from his faith and his family. The sea had been good to him, it was a familiar setting, an old friend, but somehow he knew that the time had come to say good-bye.

"How much diesel?" Mark asked, not believing what he was told.

"Sixteen hundred gallons total. I reconfirmed that number with the Lagos fuel depot. You weren't expecting to take on that much?" Captain Everlast asked.

"No, I guess I underestimated the leaks. I'm going to up the inspections, make them twice daily."

"Could we have a more serious leak elsewhere?" the Captain asked. "Some of the seals for the diesel strainers might be going bad."

"Doubtful. We're okay, Cap. I think. I will personally go below and inspect the bilge again."

"Do that. I've been told the NAV computer is nearly installed. I would like to get underway today, if possible."

One more time in his head Mark recalculated the amount of diesel fuel *The Star* should have needed to top off the generators' tanks. He was right; they should have needed only six hundred gallons at most in the six thousand gallon tanks. They had only been at sea for a short time since refueling. A thousand gallons or more of fuel was unaccounted for, which was a very unpleasant prospect.

Fuel does not just disappear or vaporize in the tank. The only conclusion Mark could reasonably draw was that somewhere on *The Star* a large pool of diesel fuel was sitting around just waiting to ignite.

"Evan," Mark asked as he reached the Generator Room, "when is the last time you inspected the bilge?"

"Yesterday, oh eight hundred, Sir."

"Any sign of leaks?"

"Sheen on the water, but nothin' serious enough to cause concern. Why?"

"We are re-inspecting the bilge right now."

"Problem?"

"Let's hope not."

"Hold up a sec, Mark. Herman's finishin' up repairin' that loose railing, you know on the other side of the ..."

Mark looked up and saw what he feared. He could see welder sparks flying from behind the second generator.

"What did I tell you Evan! No welding or sparks down here unless you..."

"I inspected the bilge. No oil or diesel."

"Come on. Herman can find something else to do for a while until we re-inspect."

After only a few steps Mark could smell it, the unmistakable odor of diesel fuel. It was coming from below. My God! Now he ran as fast as he could toward Herman, who was completely focused on his work.

Mark was seconds too late.

As if in slow motion, Mark watched as the sparks from Herman's welder drifted through the grating near the second generator and fell into the bilge below.

With a loud "whoomph" the diesel fuel ignited sending tongues of flame shooting up though the grating at several points in the Generator Room.

Evan pulled the alarm. Herman turned off his welder and dropped it as he jumped away from the open flame.

"Herman, grab the CO_2 extinguishers! They're right over your head!" Mark yelled.

A rack of four fire extinguishers was covered by a glass plate. Openia broke the glass with a wrench from his tool kit, grabbed all four extinguishers and passed them out to Mark and Evan.

"Doesn't the bilge have a fire suppression system?" Evan yelled.

Mark was thinking the same thing. The flames were still too intense to actually look in the bilge through the small grated openings beneath the generators. He could hear what he thought was a high pitched hissing from the release of water or halon into the bilge area. But whatever was happening down there, the flames were not going out.

"Herman! Pry open a piece of that decking, as far away from the motor generators as you can get!" Mark ordered.

As Herman was doing that, Evan and Mark used iron bars to remove the grated plates beneath both generators. They had to do this quickly and carefully, flames were leaping at them and singeing the bottom of the still running generators. Once the grates were off, they blasted the bilge beneath the generators with CO2 from the extinguishers.

"Mark! I made a hole!" Herman yelled.

"Spray it!" Mark shouted back.

The fire crew arrived just as Mark and Evan's extinguishers were nearly spent.

Captain Everlast was leading the fire crew. He barked his first order, "Kill the generators!"

Mark used a pair of gloves to pull the emergency stop lever for generator number one. Some of the lights flickered as the automatic transfer switches did their jobs and the load was transferred to generator number two. With generator one now shut down, the entire ship was being fed from the second generator.

. When Mark moved to the second generator, where Evan was still busy pouring CO2 into the bilge below, he knew that he was in trouble. Fire was trickling up the side of the generator, obviously finding a new fuel source. It wasn't hard to figure out; caked oil on the bottom of the engine was igniting.

Mark pushed Evan aside, afraid that Evan was standing too close to the flames for his safety. As he pulled the emergency stop lever on the second generator Mark noticed that the bottom of the engine was completely aflame, white hot like a pan on a stove.

Pulling the emergency lever did not stop the second generator. Captain Everlast was watching Mark as he tried again to cut off the engine to no avail.

"Get outta there Schaefer, right now!" Captain Everlast shouted.

Mark could see that it was hopeless. The heat from the fire had caused a diesel engine runaway - a rare condition where the engine races out of control, consumes its own lubrication oil and runs at higher and higher RPMs until it overspeeds to a point where it destroys itself either due to mechanical failure or engine seizure through lack of lubrication.

The fire crew, dressed in their Kevlar suits and rubber boots, now began pouring CO_2 into the air intake of the engine, desperately trying to smother it.

So much CO_2 was in the air, along with the burning diesel and exhaust, that it was impossible to breathe. Mark grabbed a respirator just in time, but he looked over and Herman and Evan were passed out of the floor. Before he could reach his friends, members of the fire crew were on them pulling respirators over their faces and moving them to safety. The Captain and Mark remained, along with the five man fire crew.

The second generator was running at over six thousand RPMs now, whining like a geyser about to erupt.

"Could it explode, Captain?" Mark asked, as he raised his respirator and shouted in Everlast's ear.

"No, but it's history. The generator is destroyed. Pretty quick here it will simply seize and that will be it."

A few minutes later, as the flames from the bilge fire began to subside, the huge motor generator seized with a loud bang, scaring the heck out of everyone in the Generator Room. Exhaust fans had removed most of the CO_2 from the air. It was clear that the worst was over; although the fire crew would have to spend hours making sure that every last bit of flame was suppressed before repairs could begin.

They were on ultra-emergency power now. Fans replaced air conditioning and batteries were powering emergency lighting throughout the ship.

Captain Everlast and Mark removed their respirators.

"I guess we found the diesel fuel," Captain Everlast said.

"Herman set it off, Cap. He didn't mean to, I had issued a standing order not to use welding equipment down here but ..."

"I will file a full report after an investigation, but we all knew about the fuel leak problem. It was well documented. I will not make Herman a scapegoat."

"Blame me, Cap."

"Stuff happens, Schaefer! Climb down off your cross! You've got a lot of work to do," Everlast barked.

"Yes sir." Mark knew that he had a bad habit of always trying to be "Papa Bear" and protecting people from the consequences of their mistakes. But Cap was right. Sometimes things happen. The true cause of the accident was not a lack of diligence on his part or the crew, but rather a lack of required scheduled maintenance. The fuel lines leading to the generators should have been replaced eighteen months earlier.

As the fire crew was winding up their efforts, Mark felt it was safe for him to go topside and get some air. He knew that Keith would be worried about him and waiting for him to emerge from the charred wreckage of the Generator Room.

"You okay, my brother?" Keith said, handing Mark a bottle of water.

Mark downed the bottle in three gulps. Keith handed him another one which he also poured down his throat as if he hadn't had a drink in days.

"Your arm. Mark," Keith said, as he grabbed Mark's right forearm.

"Man! I never felt a thing," Mark said.

Mark's arm was burned from elbow to wrist and it looked like it might be a second degree wound.

"You're going to medical. Now!" Keith said, almost like an order.

Mark smiled, but didn't argue. He was glad that Keith was looking after him. On the way to see the doctor, Mark said a silent prayer thanking God that no one was seriously hurt and the fire was over.

Nine

Forty five minutes, a few aspirin and a bottle of saline later, Mark was bandaged up with sterile dressing and ready to trouble shoot. Fixing problems was Mark's specialty, his greatest strength. Captain Everlast was counting on him.

"You're sure that you can get the generator working within a few hours?" Everlast asked.

"Positive, Cap. Well, how about a definite

maybe," Mark said with a confident wink and a smile. "We will run it through its paces. We can't trust those old fuel lines so I'll run a temporary line above the grates from the tank directly to the generator. It won't be up to OSHA standards, but I'll flag the area so no one trips. You know my motto 'back on line, on time, every time'."

"That's good, because if you can't fix the generator, we are dead in the water. I would hate to beg for help in the middle of Lagos harbor. Corporate won't be thrilled if our little mess becomes public knowledge." Captain Everlast paused and then asked a question, "How confident are you that the generator will keep working during the voyage home?"

"Seventy five to eighty percent certain. There was a lot of heat down there. I mean I will check everything as best as I can, but you never really know. The generator could have been damaged in ways I can't detect. It definitely needs an overhaul."

"If we lose electrical power at sea Mark, well, that'll be a horrible mess."

"Been through that once Cap, I'll pass on doing it again."

"We will have an escort. We won't be in any danger."

"Are we off loading the crude?"

"Have to. At least we found a convenient place to break down. The Lagos terminal can take our load; the company will basically do a swap out later. That part is no big deal."

"I still can't believe we had a bilge fire. Of all things couldn't it..."

"Your quick action saved generator number one. If you had hesitated it might have cooked too."

"Newburg pointing fingers yet?"

"Only at themselves. They know they can't fault anyone on this vessel. Those lines should have been replaced months ago; only they are to blame for that. Now they are minus a generator. That'll add a cool half a million to their bill," Everlast said.

"Okay. Anything else sir?" Mark asked.

"What's this I hear about you quitting?"

"Sir?"

"Don't be mad at Evan. He thinks you walk on water. He was going on to Keith about how glad he was that you were still here and I just happened to be standing behind him."

"Cap, I...it's not certain yet. But my family, you know, they need me. I have to start thinking about getting a land job."

"I understand. Take your time. It's not easy to find the same pay on dirt as you enjoy at sea."

"You're the best, Cap. I mean it."

"I won't say anything to anybody else."

"I'll get back to work then, sir."

"*The Florida Star.* Complete five year maintenance package, plus a new generator. Huge coup, Mike. Well done," Billy Caesar complimented.

"Doesn't mean a thing," Michael Patty groused.

Billy Caesar, the General Manager of St. John's Shipyard and Michael Patty, his Sales and Marketing Head, were sitting in Caesar's office reviewing the maintenance contract Patty had just closed with Newburg to repair *The Florida Star*.

"A couple of mill net in Bowman's pocket doesn't mean a thing?"

"Will they pull back their bulldog? No. Will he still fire all of us and ruin this shipyard? Yes. Like I said, it doesn't mean a thing."

"It might save some jobs for a few months, anyway. Campo can't fire the whole crew and expect to complete all that work on an Aframax tanker," Billy said.

"That's the only reason I cut the deal with Newburg. The *only* reason. After *The Star* is gone, so am I, Billy."

"Mike, slow down. We haven't played the last card yet."

"What card do we have left to play?"

Billy Caesar scratched his well-trimmed grey beard and took another sip of coffee. He knew that Mike was right, Bowman Industries seemed bent on getting rid of every manager associated with Larken. Bowman's Vice President, Jabber Campo, who was sent down by corporate to oversee all operations, had made it clear from his first day on the job that "he was here to ensure that St. John's Shipyard becomes a highly profitable operation". For the past few weeks Campo had droned on and on about how Andy Larken had "run this Yard like an amateur", and "needlessly paid way too much" for this and that, while he "ridiculously overspent" on purchasing duplicative backup systems and favored the union whenever they asked for a concession.

Billy Caesar and Mike Patty knew that there was

some truth in Campo's rants. Andy Larken did not consider the Yard's bottom line to be the only, or even the most important, measure of its success. St. John's Shipyard was known in the industry as the most solid, honest and reliable facility on the east coast. It wasn't the most modern in terms of equipment or technology, or the largest, or the best capitalized, but if your vessel fit in the Yard's dry docks and the work could be done at St. John's, you knew that everything would be taken care of properly, on time and within budget. .

St. John's had a very impressive client list. That is the primary reason why Bowman Industries bought the Yard. Yet Jabber Campo seemed intent on destroying the very asset his company paid for, the goodwill of St. John's customers.

Bowman's modus operandi was simple – underbid their competitors to get the job and then pressure the customer to sign off on extra work or unforeseens to the contract. While this tactic was not uncommon in the industry, even expected in most quarters, it made Mike Patty's stomach turn.

Patty had to reassure his longtime industry contacts that everything at St. John's was the same under Bowman as it had been under Larken and that they could still rely on the same exceptional level of honesty, quality and customer service they came to expect for decades under Andy's leadership.

Trouble was, Mike's reassurances were close to becoming bold faced lies. As long as he and Billy were around they believed that they could finagle things to be sure that work was properly done, but they both knew that the axe could fall on their heads at any moment.

Mike Patty was old school. Integrity, family, relationships and honor were everything to him; as he often said, "What else is there?" While he liked to drink some and was well known as the man to see for a good time, Mike's word was his bond. After *The Star* left, he would too because he simply refused to be made into a liar.

Billy's phone rang. He answered it and said, "He's in here. Okay, you bet."

"Campo is walking down the hall. He needs to speak with you," Caesar said.

"Can I climb out the window?" Mike asked, half jokingly.

"Come on, Mike. Hang in there."

"I'm too old to 'hang in there'. What say we give the him a knuckle sandwich and email Bowman New

York with our resignations?"

"Mike."

"Okay, okay. I'll play nice."

The door to Billy Caesar's office opened without a knock. Campo walked into the room like it was his office. He glared at Mike and then proceeded to sit down in the guest chair at the desk.

"Mike, what the heck is this?" Campo said, pointing to page thirty of the contract Patty had just signed with Newburg for *The Florida Star*.

"I'm lost, Jabber. As usual," Mike curtly responded.

"I told you that we needed a thirty percent margin on the generator. You bid fifteen percent. Why on earth would ..."

"We don't pad equipment costs thirty percent, Jabber. Blame me. I approved the number," Billy interjected.

"You think this is charity, Caesar? I told you ..."

"Newburg has been a customer of this yard for twenty-five years. They go out of their way to bring ships to us even if it costs them more than a bit more to get them here. You know why, Jabber? They trusted Andy and they trust me and Billy. They know that they can rely on our integrity. We do not pad equipment costs by thirty percent."

"Well, now you do. Everything gets marked up thirty percent. That's the minimum by the way, not the ceiling. We will bring labor costs down and very soon. That's where we can cut our bids. Am I making myself clear?"

"Very clear," Mike said, almost snarling.

"Hey Patty, if you don't like what we're doing here then walk. I told you that some ..."

"Listen to me, Campo. I love this Yard and care about my customers. I spent twenty years building on the work done by the men who came before me. We created an ..."

"You created an asset that was purchased for a fair price. Bowman Industries owns this facility now and we will run it as we see fit. I appreciate your contacts and reputation. You work hard, I'll give you that. But you will get with the program or you will find somewhere else to practice your 'integrity'."

Billy could see that Mike Patty was done. If he let him Mike would walk, right now, before or after punching Jabber Campo on the jaw. He could not let that happen.

Billy stood, walked around his desk and put his

hand on Mike's shoulder. Then he said, "We understand, Jabber. From now on all bids get approved by you before they are sent to the customer. Will that satisfy you?"

Campo was busy giving Mike Patty a look that said, "Go on, cowboy. I dare ya. Make my job easier."

For a minute no one said a word. Jabber knew something that Mike and Billy did not - Bowman New York had given Campo orders to keep the existing top management structure at the Yard in place for another six months. If they quit, they quit, but Campo had no authority to fire either Mike or Billy.

"Fine. Look, we need to work together. The goal here is to maximize the profit of this Yard, gentlemen. I'm not here to make friends; I'm here to make money. Please keep that in mind."

After Camp finished his trite little speech, he got up from the chair and walked to the door. He turned around one last time to glare at Mike and Billy. He said nothing else as he rolled out of the office and slammed the door behind him.

"How, or better still, why am I still employed?" Mike asked as soon as Campo was gone.

Billy was asking himself the same thing. "Maybe

he can't fire us," Caesar guessed.

"If that's true then let's do whatever we can to make his life miserable," Mike said, more than half seriously.

"You asked me what other card we had to play. Maybe that's it. For a while anyway we might be immune to his machete."

"That would be worth staying a bit more for, a free pass to annoy Jabber Campo. Okay, I'm re-energized. I'll do my best to think up ways to make him mad."

"Easy there, Michael. Help me with *The Star*. Keep Newburg happy; you're great at that, indispensable. Who knows, maybe Jabber will mess up and give us an opening. I know Bowman's CEO, William Langston. He's a New York suit, but not a complete fool."

"Do me a favor?" Mike Patty asked.

"Name it," Billy answered.

"Just find some way to keep that Jabber out of my sight. Do that and I will try to help."

"I'll do everything I can, my friend. I'll take all the heat."

"Next time he smarts off to me...well. What can I say? You've known me for twenty years, Billy."

Mike Patty's reputation as a good natured Irishman with a bad temper was well known around the Yard. Twice over the past two decades Billy had to bail Mike out of jail, both on the same charge, simple assault.

Caesar knew very well that Patty had his limits. He wondered if Jabber knew that or even cared.

After Mike left his office with a quick joke and a smile, Billy Caesar said to an empty room, "We sure miss you Andy. How 'bout tossin' us down a little help?"

Ten

Twenty two days after leaving Lagos, *The Florida Star* arrived at the Port of Jacksonville, Florida. The mighty St. John's River, being one of only two rivers in the world that flowed North, was originally named '*The River May*', after Jean Ribault discovered it in May of 1562.

Mark Schaefer had made the right call; the singed generator steadily produced electrical power all the way to America. The small escort ship that had accompanied *The Star* on its voyage from Africa now moved north toward Charleston, South Carolina.

"It's good to be home," Mark said, as he and Keith watched *The Star* maneuver itself into the St. John's Yard from the port side rail.

"Is Joy waiting for you on the dock?" Keith asked.

"As always. I'm sure glad my burned arm healed as fast as it did. What about Megan, is she waiting on the dock?"

"No. I told her that I needed to go home, get settled and then I'd call her."

"Trying to keep some distance?"

"Yea. I made an appointment with a Pastor. I want to talk with him, tell him about my situation and get some sound advice."

"Keith, that's just what you should do. Good decision."

"Do you have any job interviews lined up?"

"A couple. Joy did some calling around; can't say I'm too excited about either opportunity."

"Mark, I know you need to be home with your family but the sea, man, it's your life. I just can't imagine you anywhere but aboard ship."

"Better start imagining it. I have to change, things have to change. My family comes first."

The Star navigated the short distance up the St. John's River toward the Yard and waiting dry dock. The Harbormaster's pilot was on board and he was now guiding *The Star* in along with Captain Everlast.

The dry dock, *Andrew Jackson,* was one of the largest floating dry docks in the United States, capable of handling ships up to forty feet longer than *The Star*. General Andrew Jackson, hence the name Jacksonville, sent a former Governor of Georgia, John Forsyth, to France, thus forging the Louisiana Purchase or future of America. Truly Jacksonville is a historical crossroads. The depth of the St. Johns River has always been between thirty-six to forty-two feet, depending on the tide. Recently, ACD Marine had dredged the river to a new depth of forty-three to forty-six feet.

A dry dock is a type of pontoon used for one purpose, the dry docking of ships. Floodable buoyancy chambers and a "U" shaped cross section made up the structure. High wing walls were used to give the massive dry dock stability when the floor or deck was below the surface of the water. When valves were opened the chambers filled with water causing the dry dock to float lower in the water. The deck then submerged, so a ship could move into position inside. Once positioned over keel blocks (the material that holds the ship up ten feet or so above the deck), water was pumped out of the chambers, the dry dock rose and the ship was lifted out of the water.

A typical floating dry dock has multiple, rectangular sections. The *Andrew Jackson*, when fully utilized, had five separate sections. Each section contained its own equipment for emptying the ballast. Access to all spaces within each section was provided to complete required services.

"Are we ready, Harry?" Billy Caesar asked Harry Reed, the Head of Maintenance at the Shipyard.

"Think we are boss. Float it," Harry responded.

Caesar followed all of the protocols and when his checklist was complete he ordered the dry dock to fill its sections with pressurized air. Slowly the huge tanker rose out of the water, exposing its twin screws and scarred hull below the water line. It took less than twenty minutes for *The Star* and the Yard to give the all clear. *The Florida Star*, all 230 meters of her, was now perched on its keel blocks waiting for the maintenance crews to begin their work early the next morning.

"Baby," Joy said, giving Mark a deep, passionate kiss. "I love you. We are so glad that you're home." Fletcher, barely twelve, always had a hard time for the first few minutes when he saw his Dad again after a three month or longer absence. A bit shy, he hung back as Joy and Chrissy smothered Mark with affection.

"What about you, son? Don't I get a hug?" Mark teased.

Fletcher sighed, the way he always did, and looked down at the ground as he slowly inched his way toward his father. Mark scooped him up and gave him a big hug. That was all Fletcher needed. He wrapped his arms around his father's neck and refused to let go, as if only his firm grip was keeping Mark from getting back on board ship and leaving again.

"Keith," Joy said, as she gave Keith Toms a quick peck on the cheek.

"Joy," Keith said warily, knowing what was coming next.

"Please don't get Mark killed, okay? The kids and

I kinda need him," Joy gently scolded.

"I'll do my best," Keith said, hanging his head. "I'm really sorry, Joy. I had no idea that ..."

"You don't have to explain anything to me, Keith. We love you like family. Just be careful, please."

"Yes ma'am." Keith treated Joy as if she was his older sister and deferred to her with respect.

"Daddy, can we go to the beach tomorrow? It's supposed to be real warm even though it's only May," Chrissy asked.

"Wanna cook some dogs and go body surfing?" Mark asked.

"Yes please," Chrissy answered in a delighted tone.

"I can't wait to spend the whole day with the kids. What a blessing."

The Shipyard Workers Union was a part of the larger AFL-CIO affiliated International Brotherhood of Boilermakers. Since before World War II, St. John's had been a union yard, although not strictly so. Smaller jobs and specialty projects were often done with independent labor. There had not been one strike or any major labor tension between the Larken family and the workforce from 1935 to the present day. Back in the day, the U.S Navy mothballed its WWII fleet in Green Cove Springs, Florida, until President Johnson transferred all the ships to Houston, Texas.

All that changed in the blink of an eye when Bowman sent Jabber Campo down to oversee the St. John's.

Florida is a 'right to work' state. In theory, this meant that a person did not have to be a union member to work at the Yard. Andy Larken knew that he was legally free to hire workers from outside of the union, but he rarely did and not for entirely unselfish reasons. Anyone who did not treat his position as a member of "Larken's Team" with the proper respect was swiftly dealt with by the shop stewards. Management never had a tough time getting rid of the occasional bad apple employee, because the union supported proper discipline. Larken always made his labor decisions after consulting with the shop stewards. Multi-year labor contract negotiations were often more cordial than combative.

Although Andy Larken was gone, the Shop Stewards still wielded real power on the Yard, as did the Business Agent. The workers elected a new Business Agent right after Bowman Industries bought St. John's, replacing a "lap dog" with a "Rottweiler", correctly assuming that Bowman's goal was to try and bust the union. Frank George, the new Business Agent, was now the man on the hot seat.

"All five new hires refused to join," George said, reporting to the assembled meeting of the local. "No doubt that was part of the deal – if you want a job, you can't join the union."

"Forget that!" an unhappy member shouted. "That's illegal."

"Tough to prove," Frank George continued. "I think we should expect that every new hire will refuse to join."

"What about Grimaldi and Hansen?" another member shouted.

"They are ex-employees, although both intend to sue for wrongful termination."

"This is garbage!" shouted an angry man.

"Yea, the heck with Bowman!" screamed another.

It was an ugly scene. Many of the men had been

drinking, and they were itching for a fight. Threats of sabotage were now being openly made. Jabber's life was being threatened.

"Gentlemen! Gentlemen! Please!" Frank George hollered through a bull horn. "Listen to me!"

No one paid attention, the tumult grew worse.

"Hey! Shut up!" Frank George barked through his fully amplified bull horn. He played with the settings on the horn and produced an ugly, angry screech.

That did it. People stopped screaming at each other, if only temporarily.

"All this bravado is useless, men. I have a real plan, a way to send Bowman a message without damaging any property or getting us tossed in jail," George said, as calmly as possible.

The crowd went nearly silent, all eyes were on Frank.

"*The Florida Star* went into the *Jackson* dry dock today, as everyone knows. Bowman is counting on the revenue from this maintenance contract to provide most of their second quarter income. A new generator needs to be installed and that means opening up the side of the ship. They need skilled labor to do this; they could not replace us all quickly enough if we walked out. Newburg would simply refloat the ship and take it elsewhere if there was a strike."

"Well, what's the angle then?" a man from the crowd asked.

"We slow our pace down to an annoying crawl. We follow a schedule; everyday no more than half of us will show up for work, the rest of us will call in sick. Those that are here will work at a leisurely, but not completely stalled, pace. Then, I hope and pray, Bowman New York will see that things are close to getting out of control down here. They'll know what we're doing is deliberate, but if men use only the sick leave they've got coming and some work still continues, we put Jabber Campo on a hot plate."

"A kinda sick-out?" another man asked.

"We show Bowman that all we have to do is take the next step and *The Star* will be gone. I will find a way to communicate with the right execs in New York. I'll tell them that if they get rid of Jabber and stop trying to bust our balls they can make some money here."

"What if they just lock us out? Bring in scabs?" someone else asked.

"They could do that, but they'd lose *The Star*. That's our leverage," Frank George replied.

"*The Star* is just one ship, one contract," a man noted.

"All we are trying to do is to get those suits up in New York to realize that while we know Andy and his family are gone forever we can work with them too; make some changes, do things their new way. If we cross the line and start sabotaging equipment or beating people up we lose all credibility. Does everyone here understand that?"

A murmur of disgruntled groans and whispering indicated that Frank had driven his point home.

"Alright then. Play this out. This is *our* Yard. They might have the deed, but we've put our blood, sweat and souls into this property. Andy built this place with us, not in spite of us. Before we quit on what was the best Yard in the country, let's try and convince Bowman that they are better off with us than without us."

Frank's speech had its desired effect. The men were by no means confident, but they were determined. Maybe Bowman New York would see the light, see the obvious.

Then again, maybe not. Men like Jabber Campo deliberately left mayhem in their wake. Perhaps the only way to deal with Jabber was to get rid of him the hard way, to deal with him harshly, to give him what he deserved.

Eleven

"We've got problems, Billy," Harry Reed said, as he walked into Caesar's office and shut the door behind him.

"No kidding. Only half the men came in again today?" Billy asked.

"Yea, that's a problem. I should have said we have a new problem."

"Wonderful. As if I needed ..."

"Jessica is headed our way, apparently."

"Who is Jessica? Another suit from New York? Why don't they tell me ..." "Don't you watch the news?" Harry asked.

"Rarely."

"Jessica is a category two hurricane. She smashed into Jamaica first thing this morning. Latest models predict that there is a seventy five percent chance that the storm barrels up the coast in four days and creams us."

"My God. A direct hit, Harry?"

"That's what they're saying."

"What time is it?"

"Seven thirty."

"Everyone is gone. Does Campo know about this?"

"If he does he hasn't said a word to me about it."

Billy Caesar got up from his desk and looked out his window. His office was on the top floor of the tower, a ten story building that had a clear view of the entire Yard. The Andrew *Jackson* was a hundred yards away. He stared for a moment in the late twilight at the massive tanker perched in the dry dock.

"Harry, do you think that ..."

"Come on, Billy. This is a no brainer. We have to refloat *The Star*. At least we have four days to get her out of here. Did they open up her hull to replace the generator?"

"Yea, that was the last thing they did today. It should have been done three days ago."

"Well I know they haven't moved the new generator onto the dock yet because it's still in the warehouse. So, let's close up the hull. *The Star* can leave no later than tomorrow night."

"I have no authority to refloat *The Star*. Campo alone makes those calls."

"Okay, get him in here then. This isn't a hard decision, even for him."

Although it was late, Jabber was still in his office doing his best to placate William Langston via Skype. New York knew that Campo's methods were an extended process so they did not expect instant results. That said, some in the corporate brain trust, including CEO Langston, had doubts about their decision to use Jabber Campo's rough house tactics as the means to integrate the St. John's Shipyard into Bowman Industries.

Langston knew that they had not purchased a

broken business, just one that needed some adjustments, a few tweaks. Bowman's Board of Directors definitely wanted the union gone. That was the model that worked for them most consistently. It was certainly possible to pursue this strategy in Florida, at least from a legal perspective. But was it the best move? Consensus had not been reached in New York, the jury was still out.

Labor issues aside, Langston knew that Campo was a jerk, plain and simple. No one liked to be around the man, even those who admired his skills as a "take no prisoners" acquisition integration specialist.

The doubts in New York were increasing. The labor force at St. John's was in a half sick-out, slowdown mode. An AFL-CIO big shot from Chicago had left Langston three messages over the past forty eight hours all saying the same thing, "We need to talk about St. John's".

As Frank George had hoped for and predicted, Jabber Campo was indeed on the hot seat.

As soon as Campo finished his call with Langston, Caesar buzzed him and asked him to come to his office for a meeting. Jabber swore, grabbed his note pad and lumbered down the hall. He was in a foul mood.

"Jabber," Caesar said, greeting his boss.

"What's so urgent?" Campo bellowed.

"Jessica is moving up the coast. The latest models predict that she will nail us. We have maybe four days; two at the least, five at the most," Harry explained.

"So?" Jabber said, dismissively. "I watched the news last night. The storm is in Jamaica right now. Models...the only thing certain about them is that they are always wrong."

"You understand, right? Do I need to pull out The Dock Master's Manual and spell it out for you? High winds, big waves, storm surge, extreme tides – those things are bad news for dry docks. If we leave *The Star* with a gaping hole in her hull sitting on the *Jackson* and we get ..."

Campo looked both bored and angry, if such a state was possible. He definitely believed that Reed and Caesar were wasting his time.

"Whoa there Billy. Hold up," Jabber said, interrupting. "First of all, you don't know that we're going to get hit. That's a guess."

"I can't believe we are having this conversation.

Do you know the first thing about running a shipyard, Campo?" Harry asked, with venom.

"Yes. The first thing is that someone is always in charge. That would be me. So why don't both of you old women settle down, grow a set and tell me how we are going to ride this storm out."

"You're an idiot," Harry Reed said, as he rose and walked toward the door. "You deal with this stupid man, Billy. He's too much for me." Reed left in a lather, slamming the door behind him.

"Well?" Jabber said, looking at Billy. "I need options, not temper tantrums."

"There are no options, Jabber. We need to patch the hole and refloat the ship. That's it, plain and simple."

"No, here's what's "it", plain and simple. *The Star* is not going anywhere. We need her to stay in place and for the work to continue as scheduled."

"Newburg will be ringing your phone, Jabber. They will demand that their ship be moved out of harm's way. Expect that phone call."

"No, you expect that phone call Billy because you will be the one taking it and telling them that there is no need to panic."

"It's just one ship for a few days, Jabber. Why

would you..."

"I will not be bullied by a bunch of welders and wrench monkeys. *The Star* stays and furthermore you need to get your work crew back up to full strength."

"How can I force anyone to report for work?"

"Replace them. Half the workforce is gone, so hire enough skilled men to bring us back up to full strength."

"You can't go down to the day labor place and just pick up people with the skills we need to ..."

"I can have all the skilled labor you need here in twenty four hours."

"Scabs? Union busters? You want the union gone that bad? Why?"

"If this sick-out junk goes on even one more day, tell your friends that I will sack the lot of them, lock them out and hire a whole new crew."

"Please don't ask me to ..."

"Forget it, Caesar. I'll handle everything. You just sit in here and...Well, do whatever it is you do. *The Star* stays. Any more nonsense and the work force goes. If they think I'm kidding, just keep playing games and see what happens."

Jabber was enraged. His face was fully flushed.

He pulled himself out of the chair and walked out the door huffing and puffing all the way.

Billy was dumbfounded. There was just no other way to describe his state of mind. He kept replaying the events over and over again in his head. How could Campo possibly hope to keep *The Star* in port? Newburg owned the ship, not Bowman. How many lies did Campo think he could tell?

"What in the world is going on?" Billy Caesar asked an empty office.

Twelve

Roger drank. That seemed to be what he did best. The other thing Roger Cerrone did was pilot a barge from Jacksonville, usually to points south and back again moving cranes and dredging equipment for a third generation, family owned North Florida shipping company.

While his Coast Guard Barge Pilot record was clean, that was only because he had been given a couple of breaks. Twice he had tested positive for alcohol after delivering his cargo to either Miami or Tampa. His blood alcohol level was low each time, .06 or less, so the testing officer let him slide with a warning. Roger had clearly not been drinking on the job, but rather drinking heavily the night before. Such indiscretions were often overlooked, especially when the person being tested was well liked and had a good reputation for doing his job professionally and safely.

But tonight was different. Roger's wife, Julie, came home earlier in the day and announced that she had decided to leave him and move in with an OBGYN she nursed for on a regular basis. As it turns out, Julie had been giving extensive after care to her physician lover for over a year. He left his wife, so Julie left Roger. She was in love. Roger was devastated.

When he was upset, Roger drank even more. He knew that he was scheduled to pilot a barge later in the day from Jacksonville north to Charleston, an unusual run for him. Ships were leaving Jacksonville in a rush, hoping to avoid Jessica's wrath.

Roger not only drank, he took a few Valium. He told himself that he needed to calm down, relax, settle in. Roger knew that he was unfit to drive to the dock, much less pilot a ship. If he was tested pre-boarding he would be suspended without pay and not allowed to work. But the odds of that happening today were remote because the Coast Guard was busy managing all the traffic bugging out of Jacksonville. Routine sobriety tests were likely a very low priority.

After a hot shower, half a pot of coffee and a few dozen Altoids, Roger Cerrone was convinced that he showed no visible signs of intoxication. He was very good at hiding his addiction. He'd been doing so for over fifteen years, with near complete success.

As Roger was going through his pre-trip routines he started to feel the effects of the Valium. He almost fell asleep every time that he was not actively engaged in a task. He silently asked himself, can I do this? On some level at least, Roger Cerrone considered himself to be a diligent skipper. Years ago he vowed that he would never pilot a vessel if he was too inebriated to do so. He had never made the decision to walk away from his duties before, but tonight he had to admit to himself that he may have crossed the line. He was simply not alert enough and his reflexes were too slow.

Then he saw it, a twelve ounce can of a popular energy drink. Another crew member from the last run must have left it behind. He had never tried one before, but now was certainly the time.

After a few minutes the massive caffeine jolt from the drink had its desired effect. Roger was given a false sense of hope. Reinvigorated, he moved the barge away from the dock and up the river. He would have an hour or more to recover further up river as his cargo was loaded. He found two more cans of the magic elixir. He could make it, he told himself. He tried not to think about his wife, who was no doubt at that very moment allowing her physician to perform a gynecological exam.

By two a.m., as Roger was piloting the barge down river and out to sea, the energy drinks could no longer keep his metabolism going. Now he was fighting not only the effects of the alcohol and Valium, but also a rapid comedown from the caffeine rush.

Roger fell asleep at the wheel. As he drifted away into the land of nod, the barge was traveling at almost seven knots, a bit too fast. The current was helping and the tide was going out as well. A minute or two after Roger passed out, his speed increased to nearly ten knots.

If the barge stayed on course and did not make the required turn to port, it was headed straight for the dry docks at the St. John's Yard.

Straight for the *Andrew Jackson*. Straight for *The Florida Star*.

Because the maintenance crews needed a more generous than usual access to the aft of *The Star* to replace the generator, twenty feet of the bow of the tanker was protruding beyond the dry dock. This was by no means unsafe, it was routine. However, given Roger's decision to self-medicate, the bow of *The Star* now became a target and the barge, fully loaded with tons of steel beams, was approaching *The Star* like a guided missile locked on its objective.

Mark had not been back aboard *The Star* since they docked. Every night a two man skeleton crew was rotated on board to monitor systems and perform a few basic maintenance tasks. Tonight was Mark and Keith's night. After a few hours of light duty, Mark and Keith were sound asleep when the barge slammed into the dry dock and the ship at nearly four a.m.

The barge crashed into the *Jackson* and *The Star* at a forty five degree angle. The impact opened a gaping hole in the bow of the tanker as *The Star*board side of the barge punched its way through the hull. Another even larger hole was gouged into the dry dock, barely ten feet above the water line.

The impact knocked *The Star* off its keel blocks, slamming the ship into one side of the dry dock. The sound was deafening, like two massive steel doors slamming shut. Loose debris flew everywhere; it literally rained bits of metal for a few seconds.

Beneath the surface half of the mooring lines were instantly severed. The *Jackson* was now only attached to the harbor floor on one side.

"What was that?" Mark said, picking himself up off the floor.

"We were hit by something. What do we do?" Keith asked, as he wiped the blood gushing from his mouth. When he was tossed from his berth Keith slammed into a desk, breaking off a tooth.

"I gotta get to the bridge, call the Captain, he's on leave. You are on my tail. Do not leave my sight!" Mark shouted.

Roger awoke right after the collision. He slowly tried backing the barge away from the *Jackson.* As he did he heard the unmistakable sound of metal scraping against metal. Trying to remove the barge from the ship and dry dock only made the damage worse. Radioing the Coast Guard and the Harbormaster was a career buster. The current was working against him. He needed to think. Who can he call? He needed a second towboat.

During the first few minutes after the accident Mark was sure that the *Jackson* would sink. If it did, *The Star* would go down with it; given the two huge holes in its side everything lower than twenty feet above the bottom of the hull would instantly be underwater, causing millions of dollars in damage.

Alarms sounded, ships appeared, including a Coast Guard cutter. Barely twenty minutes after impact, the *Jackson* was surrounded by a small flotilla. Roger was numb but 'duty first'. He worked with a second towboat to get free. He tied off, rubbed his eyes and blew out a sigh of relief, shaking his head. How did he get this far off the course of life. His career was all he had left.

After talking with Captain Everlast, Mark was reassured that even if the dry dock and *The Star* sank, he and Keith were safe on the bridge. Although it would create one heck of a mess, they were only in eighteen feet of water. No one was below decks. So Mark and Keith sat tight, monitoring gauges and watching the show a hundred yards off their bow. With the scope and the binoculars Mark and Keith watched as Roger Cerrone was arrested, handcuffed and led onto the cutter by uniformed armed men.

Thirteen

It wasn't pretty. Jabber was thrilled to participate from a safe distance.

In New York, Bowman's Executive Committee was meeting with both in-house and outside counsel present. A representative from Germania Re, the company's umbrella insurance carrier, was also there looking very nervous.

William Langston began by saying, "Last night, at my home no less, I took a call from Royce Token over at

Newburg. He said that some executive down at St. John's called him late yesterday afternoon and told him that *The Florida Star* should not be in the *Jackson* dry dock due to the danger from the imminent storm. He also said that the 'incompetent jerk' we sent down to run the Yard was a 'disaster'. After the stuff hit the fan this morning, Royce called me back and was using terms like 'gross negligence' and 'deliberate deception' to describe our St. John's operation. He demanded to know 'what in the world I was going to do about it' and slammed the phone down in my ear."

"Let me explain, William, I just ...."

"No let me explain, Jabber. We are not looking good. No doubt the barge pilot is the proximate cause of the accident, but can you explain to me why the heck one of our own executives would call a customer and tell him that *The Star* had 'no reason' to be in the dry dock when the barge struck and that you are a 'walking disaster'?"

"May I speak?" Jabber asked, as politely as he could.

"Please," William Langston said.

"First things first. The barge pilot had a blood alcohol level of .20 and drugs in his system. He fell asleep at the wheel. I do not believe that there is any doubt about liability here. I'll bet anyone in the room a month's pay that someone somewhere let this fool slide a time or two on prior sobriety tests. So, if I were up there, William, I'd have the law dogs research this thoroughly. If we can find any previous history of alcohol use on the job by....what is his name? ... oh yea, Mr. Cerrone, then we are talking punitive damages, a huge payday."

The lawyers all nodded their heads in concurrence.

"As for the whole Jessica hurricane angle, our drunken barge pilot rendered the whole point moot. The dry dock took a hit too. For the moment, and we have an emergency crew working feverishly to repair the *Jackson*, the ship is stable, the dry dock is stable. Just barely, granted, but stable. The holes in *The Star*'s hull and the holes in the dry dock have rendered it impossible to move either vessel. We are in place, gentleman, we have to ride out the storm.

"Divers have not only repaired the severed mooring cables, they've added six more around the *Jackson* for added stability. We adjusted the ballast in the dry dock to account for the shift of *The Star* to one side. The *Jackson* is floating with almost no list. We are within the two percent tolerance list meter, otherwise the whole rig could flip."

"The latest models show Jessica may be headed out to sea. There is a better than 50-50 chance that the storm will pass by Jacksonville, giving us a glancing blow at worst. As long as we maintain less than a two percent list, that is"

"Sounds like you're on top of things down there Campo," an Executive Committee member complimented.

"What about all this backstabbing business with our customer, Jabber?" Langston asked.

"That's not my responsibility," Jabber Campo boldly declared.

"What?" Langston said, not believing his ears.

"You heard correctly, that's not my responsibility."

"How do you ..."

"You tied my hands, Bill. You said that Billy Caesar and Harry Reed and the rest of the execs were off limits, that I could not fire and replace them. Therefore, they are not my responsibility."

"Now wait just a minute, Jabber. Those men work for you. Can't you control your own people?" Langston asked.

"They are not my people. I did not hire them. Both Caesar and Reed despise me and Bowman. They feel a loyalty to the Yard, whatever that means, and to the workforce."

"Then fire them," a Committee Member said, interjecting. Several others on the committee concurred as did the in-house counsel.

"Fire them," Langston reluctantly agreed.

"Done. Now they are my responsibility. I will call Newburg myself and explain the situation. Unless I've missed something, and you gentlemen are the judge of that, Bowman Industries has absolutely no choice but to keep *The Florida Star* in dry dock for the next three days at least. Our hands have been tied due to the gross negligence of a third party. Can anyone there come up with an argument opposed to this position that holds water?"

No one could. Campo's question was answered by silence.

"This stupid storm will amount to nothing. It will be an over-hyped, non-event. Trust me," Jabber said not with confidence, but with cockiness, as if somehow he could predict the weather with certainty.

Jabber's reasoning was sound. His conclusions were valid.

Langston knew this, but he was still uneasy. Truth be told, he despised the man. But, love him or hate him, Jabber was making the right call.

Yet something was still nagging at him, a gut feeling telling William Langston that another shoe was about to drop. He hoped to God that he was wrong.

"Report please," Jabber said tersely.

"The dry dock is stable, but I cannot vouch for how much more pounding she can take and stay afloat. The divers have inspected every square foot of the hull, it seems sound. But a big hit, well, it crunches metal. Things like hatches can jam after a collision, valves can stick, there is just no ...."

"Great, Reed. I get it. Anything else?"

"We have closed half the hole in *The Star* that we made to access the generator. As long as the ship is in dry dock, shore power will supply ample lighting. The rest will be sealed by midnight. As for the big gash in her bow, that's a huge job, there is no way that ..."

"Yea, got it Caesar. I know that there is no way to repair that damage before the storm arrives. Are we back at full strength? No more sick-outs?"

"We are at seventy five percent. When the men heard about the barge ramming into *The Star* they felt a sense of loyalty, they were ..."

"The ten men I bused in from Charleston, they're on the job?"

"Yes," Billy replied, "given the circumstances, our crew didn't object to..."

"Great," Campo pronounced. "You're both fired, effectively immediately. Please pack up your personal effects, turn in all your keys, all that. I want you off this property in an hour."

"You dirty dog," Harry Reed said. "You ...."

"Security," Campo said, after pushing a button on his radio.

Instantly, Campo's door opened and two large, armed security guards appeared.

"Bowman will provide each of you with a fair severance package. However, I have been asked by legal counsel to inform you both that if you have any contact with our customers or employees from this point forward not only will your severance payments be nullified, but you will also be sued. Those boys up in New York don't play, Harry. One more call to Newburg and ..."

"I called Token, you miserable prick," Billy said.

"Good to know. Have a nice life, gentlemen. Stay out of mine."

With that Jabber Campo summarily dismissed Harry Reed and Billy Caesar. He sent them packing like two bookkeepers who got caught with their hands in the cookie jar.

As the guards were escorting Caesar and Reed to their offices, they noticed at least a dozen more private security officers fanning out across the Yard. St. John's was now effectively under siege.

Jabber's confidence was peaking. Soon St. John's would provide the last victory he needed to lay claim to the Vice Chairman's slot at Bowman. Then he would never have to deal with nonsense like this again; the field assignments would become someone else's problem. He would be making a couple of million per year before bonuses. Jabber would buy the apartment of his dreams and live properly as a Manhattan resident of means.

Fourteen

"Cap," Mark said, taking the phone from Joy who had answered the call.

"I need you back on board, Mark. Sorry. Newburg is sending Token and some other guys down here. If the ship sinks in the dock, we'll need you ..."

"You don't have to apologize, Captain. It's my job. Joy understands," Mark explained.

"The storm is veering out to sea," Everlast said. "I've got the National Hurricane Weather Center storm tracking page up on my computer. It might just miss us."

"The bigger storm is brewing on the Yard," Mark offered.

"That's also why I called. I heard that St. John's fired their General Manager and Head of Maintenance last night."

"I talked with Billy Caesar this morning. He thinks things might get nasty on the Yard. Assuming *The Star* gets through this storm intact, we might be wise to patch the hole in the bow as soon as possible and get out of port."

"First things first. Can you report at thirteen hundred?"

"It's nine, Cap. I can throw on ..."

"No. Spend the morning with your family, Schaefer. One o'clock is soon enough."

"Yes sir."

Mark handed the phone back to Joy who had stood right by him in the kitchen listening to Mark's end of the conversation.

"This is all over the news," Joy said, turning up the volume on the TV.

On the TV a local reporter was discussing the barge accident and the subsequent "labor troubles" on the Yard. A few of the men were expressing their views that the new owners of the Yard were "union busters" who didn't "care about Jacksonville, their employees or even their customers". The piece ended with a short statement about Andy Larken and the long history of the St. John's Shipyard.

"Is Chrissy more cheerful this morning?" Mark asked.

"Still gloomy. Do you think we overreacted?" Joy asked.

"You told her that Jeff was off limits. Then she sneaked away to go see him anyway. What if she....I don't want to think about it. She's grounded until further notice. I will also have a talk with Jeff."

"Mark, that may not be the best idea ..."

"Babe, I'm not going to yell or hurt him or anything. I was a kid once. Heck, I could easily have been exactly in Jeff's position. But he needs to know that Chrissy is off limits. If he won't agree to that, then I have to go to his parents. This is my call, hon. You don't have to take the heat on this one, put it on my back where it belongs."

"I'm so glad you're home, honey," Joy said, as she leaned over and kissed her husband.

"Once *The Star* is safe and all this is resolved I will find a job here, sweetheart. You have my word. But right now I have responsibilities. I'm sorry if..."

"I wasn't quite through with you yet, Mr. Schaefer."

"What?"

"You don't have to report for a few hours yet, right?" Joy asked.

"Not until one."

"Then you can report back to bed for duty, Mr. Schaefer. Like I said, I wasn't quite through with you yet."

Mark smiled. Whatever "it" was Joy still had it, in abundance. Every time he was with her he was reminded just how much he adored his wife. After almost twenty years of marriage they still had the hots for each other.

"Yes ma'am," Mark teased. "Reporting as ordered."

Mark and Joy quietly slipped back into the bedroom. They put the red sock over the door knob. The kids knew what that meant – unless your hair is on fire, leave us alone.

"Who was that?" Megan asked.

"Captain Everlast. I have to report back to *The Star* in a few hours. The storm and all," Keith said.

"Okay. Keith, I know. I mean....I guess," Megan Barry stammered when she was nervous. "Thanks for not hating me. A lot of guys would ..."

He hadn't intended to do it, it just happened naturally. Keith leaned over and kissed Megan. She responded enthusiastically. A few minutes later Megan abruptly said, "Keith, I should go," and broke their embrace.

"What? Why? I mean ..."

"You've been so sweet to me. But I can tell. I feel much more strongly about you than you do about me. I'm really vulnerable right now. I ..." Megan started to cry.

"Megan," Keith said, taking her back in his arms. "I...give me a chance, will ya? I didn't realize how I would feel about you, or the baby. I'm saying ..."

Megan kissed Keith again. Their embrace soon became much more passionate.

"You know that I have to leave in a couple of hours," Keith said, as he took Megan's hand and they got up from the couch.

"That's okay. It would be..." Megan let out a deep sigh and leaned into Keith's embrace.

He was feeling very different about her since his return. The baby was part of that, but only part. Megan had not been demanding or harsh with him; rather, she was open, honest, young and sweet.

Come to think of it, Keith reminded himself, Megan had always been that way. He'd just never noticed before.

"No better cure for the blues than some whiskey," Michael Patty said, pouring himself and Harry Reed a full shot.

"It's only noon, Mike. Take it easy," Harry cautioned.

"Forget easy. Let's toast Andy. To the greatest boss anyone could ever have. God rest his soul."

"God rest his soul," Harry repeated as he tossed

back his shot.

"Let me pour you ..."

"No, one and done, Mike. Slow down! The day is young."

"Maybe, but I'm not. Young, I mean."

"I know you're not hurting for money, Mike. You live frugally, you've saved a ton. There is more to life than the Yard. Spend some time with your grandkids, play more golf, go ..."

"I'm gonna find that mean ol' prick and punch his lights out," Mike vowed, slamming a second shot.

"Why? What will that accomplish?" Harry Reed asked.

"It'll make me feel a great deal better."

"You'll get arrested."

"So?"

"Mike, we can't save the Yard. It's gone, my friend. Yea, it hurts. Don't you think I'm feeling it? Billy too? Everyone? I mean it was a great place to work, it was our home. But it's gone, Mike. We can't bring it back."

"A hundred men are going to lose their jobs, Harry. Those guys depended on us. We were supposed to ..."

"We don't know that yet, maybe ..."

"What, you haven't been told?" Mike asked.

"Told what?"

"Billy called right before you walked in. Jabber brought in twenty more scabs this morning. Flew 'em in from Baltimore or somewhere. Then he locked everyone else out. He's claiming that safety has been compromised, threats made against his life. There are two dozen rent a cops patrolling the Yard like it was a high security prison."

"Can Bowman do that? Legally, I mean? The union has an existing contract with the Yard, I know that much. He can't ..."

"He's hanging his hat on the security angle; something to do with a provision in the labor contract about the company's obligation to 'maintain a secure facility at all times' because we do work on Navy and Coast Guard warships. Campo has let it be known that he will interview all existing employees, one at a time, and consider re-hiring them piecemeal as 'temporary' workers. But they would have to come back on his terms.

"Why?" Harry asked. He'd been asking himself the same question for six months. There seemed no valid business reason for Bowman to be so belligerent. Didn't they understand what they had here? St. John's was a gem, they were destroying it on a whim.

"Like I said, Jabber doesn't need a reason. It's his way or the highway. Well, guess what. I've passed the point caring. I'm gonna teach him a lesson, so help me God."

Fifteen

Jessica barreled up the Florida east coast, as if she was desperate to move north. As she did, the storm was upgraded to a Category Three hurricane with sustained winds of over a hundred and ten miles per hour. Defying the odds, the eye of the tropical cyclone not only remained offshore as it passed Jacksonville, it moved farther out to sea.

Despite their good fortune, the crew of *The Star*

new that even a glancing blow from Jessica with her high winds and storm surge could sink the ship given its precarious perch on the damaged *Jackson* dry dock. The tanker sat awkwardly off its keel blocks and flush with the south wing wall of the dry dock. Buoyancy had been added to the heavier side and ballast removed from the lighter one to keep the trim and list within tolerable ranges. Campo had seen to it that the *Jackson* was secured in every possible way with extra mooring cables and heavy anchors. But there was only so much that could be done. If the sea turned too violent, no amount of preparation could prevent the inevitable.

Around three a.m. Jessica's winds began to whip the water in Jacksonville harbor creating four foot whitecaps backed by eight foot seas. As luck would have it, three a.m. was also low tide so as the storm increased in intensity, the tide would be moving out.

Aboard *The Florida Star* Captain Everlast, three people from Newburg's corporate office in Boston, Mark, Keith and two other crew members had prepared for the worst. The best advice they received was that if the dry dock sank, *The Star* simply would sink along with it. There would not be time to do much, but there wasn't much they could do. The bottom was silt, but solid.

Within a four hundred foot radius from the dry dock the harbor was no more than thirty eight feet deep. Before they sank it might be possible to maneuver the ship a bit, but basically it would settle in the mud, water would pour in and the damage would be done.

As dawn broke Jessica unleashed her fury. Beneath the tanker the dry dock shivered and groaned, but it held. Two feet of storm surge lashed against the pontoon and flowed over the deck of the *Jackson*. How much water crashing over the dry dock would be enough to float the ship, or move it, even if the dry dock itself remained intact? No one was sure, but it seemed unlikely that enough storm surge water could flow over the deck to float the ship, but it might cause her to shift positions on the precariously balanced dry dock, which could also be disastrous. The dry dock wing control centers were fully manned, ready to try and compensate for the movement of the ship with buoyancy and balance adjustments.

The morning moved steadily on, eight became nine then ten a.m. With each passing minute the men inside *The Star* grew more hopeful that perhaps the dry dock would hold. Jessica continued to drift farther away, sliding to the north and east.

By noon the worst was over. When the winds dropped below fifty miles per hour and the storm surge backed off to nearly negligible, Everlast declared victory. *The Star* and the *Jackson* had both been tossed around, but serious damage had been avoided.

In New York, William Langston and Bowman's Executive Committee breathed a sigh of relief. In the space of forty eight hours Jabber Campo had gone from goat to hero. Every move he'd made had seemingly been validated – the hurricane only grazed Jacksonville, the dry dock had held and the men he'd brought in to replace the locked out workers had done their job under tough circumstances.

As Jessica raged outside, inside the Boilermaker's Union hall angry men were breathing fire. They directed their wrath toward their Business Agent.

"We tried it your stupid way, George," a huge welder yelled. "And now we're locked out. It's time for action!"

It was impossible to be heard above the din. They weren't a union at the moment; they were a mob out for blood.

Campo had forced Frank George's hand. All he could do was try and be the voice of reason and keep a lid on the violence and retribution. He joined the raucous chorus, cursing Bowman Industries and Jabber Campo. Perhaps, he thought, if I show some emotion now I might gain the credibility I need to calm things down later.

In the morning the pickets would go up. Union men would have to be compelled by force to allow anyone through the gates of the Yard.

The police would get involved. Violence was now a certainty; it was just a matter of degree.

Men were going to jail. Good men, family men, who might be foolish enough to get caught up in a bad situation and do something they would later regret.

Bowman started the war, but Frank George knew that the union would surely finish it.

That scared him to death.

Sixteen

"Lieutenant?" Officer Brady asked, wanting to be sure he was making the right call.

The police were following their new routine. Twenty of the Jacksonville Sheriff's Department's finest arrived at six a.m. and watched patiently as the picketers set up their line. Precisely at eight a well-marked van with five St. John's Shipyard security guards arrived and demanded access to their place of employment, but before the guards got out of their van and the situation took a turn for the worse, the police tried to intervene.

"Go get 'em" Lieutenant Woodhead said with reluctance. "This is so futile; I mean they know....just go get 'em."

Three men had chained themselves to the front gate of the St. John's Shipyard. Unless someone wanted to break them in half, drawn and quartered style, the gates could not be opened until the men were removed.

"Ryan Brady!" shouted a picketer. "Do the right thing! Support a brother!"

Officer Brady didn't respond, but he knew the man who was hollering at him. They went to the same Church. Their kids played together.

Eggs, well past their prime, and month old tomatoes began to pelt the St. John's van. This had also become part of the sad, daily dance at the gate.

Then the picketers broke their routine. They aimed their rotten fruit and spoiled vegetables at the cops. Brady was hit first, then another man in blue. The security guards piled out of their van. It was on.

After calling for help, Lieutenant Woodhead, along with fifteen of his fellow officers, sprinted toward the front gate. In the few seconds it took them to get there, a pushing and shoving match had become a melee.

One of the picketers hit a security guard with a baseball bat. Blood splattered, but emboldened, the same picketer then took a swing at a policeman. That was all Woodhead needed to see. His men fired tear gas into the fracas. Choking men were brought to their knees. Gas masks on, the officers swooped in and began rounding everyone up. More police vehicles arrived. The three men who had chained themselves to the gate traded their self-imposed restraints for handcuffs.

The press captured the entire episode on video. Clips of the confrontation taken from phone cameras went viral on the internet as soon as they were posted.

"Stupid," Mark said, watching the battle from the safety of his living room. "Really, really dumb. All of the scabs are being shuttled in from the water. They are stopping nothing. They have to know that....why?"

"They're fighting for their jobs, Mark. It's posturing. If they're on TV, maybe they think they're winning," Joy offered.

"Winning what?"

"I don't know, baby. They're our friends. What

can we do?"

"Talk some sense into them. I don't know...I just don't see the point. They are trying to move a boulder with a crowbar. I... do you think I should report today?"

"Why wouldn't you?"

"Posturing? Show of support?"

"Now whose being foolish."

"This is so, so stupid. This Bowman outfit...what are they thinking?"

"Your ship is in that Yard, you have to go. But why the overnight bag, hon?"

"I'm going to Charleston, evidently. A two day trip, babe."

"Charleston?"

"When the Yard refloats *The Star* we are leaving, not going back on the dry dock. We are taking the ship to Charleston."

"Is this some sort of secret?"

"Yep, I wasn't supposed to tell you, but of course I'm going to tell you."

"Why not let the Yard know?"

"Newburg says it's too risky. People are afraid, you know, of sabotage. I know that sounds kinda far...."

"Not really," Joy said.

On the TV the local news was showing a close up of Officer Ryan Brady's face. Blood was streaming down his right cheek as the EMTs were busy closing up a nasty gash on his forehead.

"Man!" Mark exclaimed.

"Be careful, hon. Don't take any chances. Promise me."

"Is *The Star* patched to your satisfaction, Captain?" Jabber asked Captain Everlast.

"It is. Your men did a fine job, Mr. Campo. *The Star* is seaworthy," Everlast replied.

"Please call me Jabber, Captain."

"Mr. Campo, once *The Star* is re-floated how long do you estimate it will take your crew to inspect and repair the keel blocks?"

"I'm told no more than two hours, barring an unforeseen circumstance."

"Everything else on the *Jackson* is in order?"

"We have a small problem with one of the ballast tanks, section four. Since we need to fully submerge the

Jackson to re-float *The Star*, our men are inspecting that tank now. I think the water pipe to the pump is cracked. It's an easy swap out, a minor nuisance."

"How long will that take to resolve?"

"No more than an hour."

"Until then," Everlast said, dismissing himself with a tip of his cap.

"Until then." Jabber responded. As soon as Captain Everlast was out of earshot, Jabber finished the sentence under his breath.

Mark arrived with some of the other crew members by water, avoiding the chaos at the gate. Once onboard he began reviewing his checklist. He was headed out to sea, if only for a day. Maybe his last day.

If it was to be his last day as an oil tanker Engineer he was glad that it was a short trip up the coast. On the way to the Yard he'd called Joy and surprised her – he booked the both of them at the King George Hotel in Charleston for a couple of days. It had been a while since they'd gone off together. Joy was thrilled, especially when Mark explained that Keith volunteered to watch the kids and have a "heart to heart" with Chrissy. She would leave in the morning and meet Mark in South Carolina.

"Where's Keith?" Mark asked Evan, as he popped up on the bridge to get a progress report.

"He went and volunteered. They needed an extra hand fixin' a pipe or somethin' on the *Jackson*, so Keith said he'd go," Evan answered.

"Does the Captain know?" Mark asked.

"Cap was standin' right there when it went down," Evan replied.

"Alright." Mark was uneasy with Keith out of his sight, but he dismissed his fears as being groundless. In an hour or so he and Keith would be kicking back watching the ocean and enjoying his last ride as a merchant marine.

"How much?" Keith asked.

"Four hundred dollars a day, plus a room and per diem," Randy answered.

"For how long?" Keith wanted to know.

"Guaranteed two week contract. Beyond that, no promises."

"You realize that there are a hundred guys

marching out front who'd like to rip your head off and ..."

"Yea I, we, get that. Hey, I got a family to feed too you ..."

Suddenly the Jackson lurched, as if someone had bent it in the middle. When the dry dock jerked Keith was holding on to the ladder in the ballast tank with his right hand and had a pipe wrench in his left. He was twenty feet above the hard steel floor of the tank bottom when he lost his balance and fell to the floor. Keith began to bleed from his mouth immediately. He wasn't moving.

Randy, Pete and Rex, the three temporary scabs that were fixing the pipe with Keith, were jostled and frightened, but unhurt. They managed to hang on to something when the movement began, so they avoided a fall.

Then the *Jackson* rocked violently again; it felt like the structure was coming apart. Unconscious, Keith was tossed into the side of the tank like a rag doll.

"What the heck was that!" Rex screamed. "We gotta get out of here!"

Randy climbed down the ladder to see to Keith. He checked for a pulse and thankfully Keith still had one. But given his fall, Randy wanted permission or, better yet, an order to move him before they drug him up the ladder.

As he was reaching for his radio Randy heard, "Are you guys okay down there in Section Four Ballast? This is the dry dock north wing wall Control Room. Check in!"

Randy hit the talk key and said, "Man down! We need a medic here now. The guy is breathing, he has a pulse, but he took a serious fall. Send down a ..."

"It's stuck! The crazy hatch is stuck! Rex screamed at the top of his lungs. "We're trapped!"

"Repeat that?" the control room asked.

"Evidently the hatch from the ballast tank to the Pump Room is stuck. I haven't been up there, but one of the guys is ..."

"Sit tight, help is on the way."

"I got no problem with that," Randy told the Control Room, "but Keith here, he might."

"Report!" Captain Everlast barked over the microphone. "I want everyone accounted for, now!"

Mark was on the bridge, as were two other crew members. Evan and the others were below, but they quickly checked in. No one aboard *The Star* was hurt.

"What was that, Cap?" Mark asked.

"The dry dock is coming apart. The stress on the sections from the collision with the barge, the damage from the storm and the weight shift probably snapped a moment connection. But that's just a guess," the Captain answered.

"What on earth is a 'moment connection'?" Mark needed to know.

"Pins or plates at the top and bottom of the wings that hold the dry dock together. Too much stress and they pop like champagne corks. We may not need to be re-floated, the ..."

"Keith!" Mark suddenly remembered.

"No! Toms, he's down in the ballast tank of section four. He might be..."

Mark grabbed the phone that was directly linked to the dry dock north wing wall Control Room by a cable attached to the ship and said, "A crewman of ours is in the ballast tank of your dry dock. What is his status?"

"Who am I speaking to, please?" the voice from the Control Room said.

"What is the..." Mark was interrupted as the Captain jerked the phone from his hands.

"This is Captain Everlast, what is the condition of my crew member?"

"Sir, I believe that your crewman, Mr. Toms, has been injured in a fall. We are sending a ..."

Mark was gone from the second he heard "injured in a fall". He ran as fast as he could off the bridge and climbed down to the dry dock, ignoring Everlast's orders to stop.

God, Mark prayed as he ran, please protect my brother.

Seventeen

"Which valve?" the nervous scab worker asked.

"Do I have to come down there and hold your hand? Third row, second from the right, clockwise until it's fully open. Then third from right, fourth from the right and so on through all ten valves in the row," the Control Room barked over the radio.

Reggie was nervous and he wasn't thinking straight. He had considerable skills as welder, but he'd never worked at a shipyard before, much less on a dry dock.

"For God's sakes, today! If you don't flood those ballast tanks this dry dock is going to snap in two. See that huge ship to your right? You're about to wear it! Turn the valves!"

That did it. Reggie didn't care which valves he turned now. Turn them all he told himself. If he messed up he could always close them.

So Reggie opened all the water valves, flooding every ballast tank on the light side of the dry dock, not just the two tanks the Control Room needed him to fill.

"No...no!" Randy yelled. "Why are they flooding the ballast tank!"

Picking up Keith in one arm to get his head out of the surging water, Randy used his other arm to push send on the radio. He managed to get out, "Stop the flooding in section four" before he had to pull Keith over his shoulder and climb to avoid drowning.

Mark heard Randy's cry for help as he flew open the door to the wing wall Control Room. The panicked operator wasn't sure what to do. He was positive that he'd given Reggie the correct valves to turn. He checked his charts again. Why was section four flooding? He didn't understand.

"Which valves need to be opened?" Mark asked.

The operator repeated the same command he'd given to Reggie moments before.

"Where are those valves?" Mark asked.

"Directly below us, two hundred feet aft."

Schaefer flew out of the Control Room, slid down the rail and jumped the remaining eight feet down to the deck. When he reached the valves, he saw that Reggie was busy turning every one of the thirty valves in front of him to the open position.

"What are you doing!" Mark yelled. "That row, all those you just opened. Close them! Counterclockwise! Now!"

Reggie obeyed in a panic. The dry dock rumbled again. The water being pumped into the wrong ballast tanks was having a decidedly negative effect.

It took a few minutes, but Mark closed all the valves Reggie had mistakenly opened in a panic. The dry dock quit making noise and stopped shaking. Another temporary dry dock worker handed Mark a radio.

"Status of section four," Mark barked, hitting the send button.

"Water flow has slowed, but it's still filling. Are you sure you closed the valve?"

Mark re-checked the section four valve. It was fully closed.

"The valve is closed. Confirmed."

"Then we have a problem. The hatch is stuck, it almost fused together when the dry dock rippled. The water will ..."

Mark interrupted, hit talk and said, "Pump the water out."

"The pump is down," the operator said.

"What?"

"The pump in section four is down. We've had guys on it for the past few minutes. No one can ..."

Before he left, Mark told Reggie, "Don't touch anything. Understand?"

Reggie was little more than a bowl of jello by that point. He took off running, headed for dry land at full speed.

Mark climbed in through the open hatch in the wing wall and slid down the ladder to the Pump Room. Three men were busy trying to start the pump, but were having no success.

"What's wrong with it?" Mark asked, panting

heavily.

"I don't know. Never worked on one of these before. Have you ever..."

Mark shoved the confused scab out of the way and examined the pump. It looked like it was built when Eisenhower was President, but it was clean and obviously well cared for, or at least it had been well cared for until Bowman took over.

The pump's engine simply would not turn over. Internally something was very wrong, but there was no time to trouble shoot, diagnose, find the parts and repair the unit.

Mark called the wing wall Control Room operator again and said, "We need a back up pump in here. Now! I will disconnect the lines and ..."

"Ah," the operator said, haltingly. "We used our last backup pump last night. There are no more."

"What?" Mark said. "That's not possible. Every system has at ..."

"There are no more pumps, sir. I'll reconfirm with Campo," the operator said.

"Mark," the weak voice called out over the radio. "You there, bro?"

It was Keith. He sounded like he could barely

speak.

"I'm here, Keith. Right outside the hatch in the Pump Room."

"Please do somethin' man. I can't breathe. I need help, please."

Then another voice spoke.

"Mark this is Randy. You don't know me, but I suggest you do whatever you have to do and damn quick. I'm doin' the best I can for Keith here but Mark, he's hurt bad. I think he's bleeding inside. He needs a doctor."

"Please help him, Randy. I will get you out."

Mark put down his radio and snapped open his cell. He still had Billy Caesar on speed dial.

Eighteen

"Slow down, Mark. Harry is here. We'll figure this out," Billy said, responding to Mark Schaefer's panicked rant.

"I need a backup pump, now. Can Harry tell me where to find one?" Mark said, as slowly as he could.

"There should be pumps in the ..."

"No. All the backup pumps are either in use or not working."

"Campo. I told him that we needed at least three backup pumps at all times, he ..."

"Harry, you can cuss Campo later. Right now I need to get those men out of the tank," Mark emphasized.

"Cut 'em out," Billy said.

"The only welder big enough to do the job quickly is also down for maintenance," Mark said.

"That's not true. Use the welder in the smaller grave dry dock. Put it on a sled and wheel it over ..."

"There's no one over there, Harry! No one knows where anything is around here! They can't even open a valve without messing up! This place is basically deserted except for the men on the *Jackson*. I have maybe thirty or forty minutes here, I ..."

"I'm leaving now. Somehow get me past the front gate. I'll be there in ten minutes," Harry instructed.

Mark didn't need any more prompting. He flew out of the pump room, slid down the ladder and ran to the tower. He hoped that Jabber Campo was in his office. He prayed that he could control his emotions long enough to get the fool to open the gate and let Harry and Billy in, otherwise...

Jabber was in his office. Just when things were

moving in the right direction, his world turned upside down again.

New York was livid over the pictures being broadcast to the nation from the Yard. Bowman Industries was being villianized on national TV. Now there was a safety issue? Men trapped in a ballast tank filling with water? The union workers at the front gate were telling everyone that Bowman management's incompetence had put lives at risk.

Campo was busy trying to backpedal and rationalize to William Langston when Mark Schaefer burst into his office, two security guards right on his heels.

"I need to call you back, William," Campo said, ending the call.

"Mr. Campo, we haven't met," Mark began, "but...get the heck off of me!" Mark shoved a guard away who was trying to restrain him.

"Leave the man alone!" Campo ordered. "But stay in the room."

The guard backed off, so Mark continued, "I need you to let Caesar and Reed and whoever else they bring with them back on the Yard. They will be at the front gate in a minute. They are the only ones who know where everything is around ...."

"You're from *The Star*, right?" Campo asked, interrupting.

"Head Engineer on *The Star*, yes."

"Will you gentlemen excuse us please?" Campo said to the guards. The guards left as instructed.

"I am working on this, Mr. Schaefer. I have forty men and equipment being flown into Jacksonville with all the equipment we need. They land in thirty minutes; they will be here in an hour. The men in the tank will be home for dinner."

"They don't have that much time. My shipmate Keith is down there. He was helping your men at their request. He fell when the dock moved, he's bleeding internally. We need to get out him out of there, *now*."

Jabber looked at Mark and then at his phone. His lines were all lit up again. New York, the press, everyone wanted a piece of him at the moment. He needed to focus, to solve the problem.

"My people tell me that the men in the tank are not in any danger from the water. We have a couple of hours at least. I don't know about your friend's medical condition, I'm truly ..."

"Are you listening, Campo? We can cut them out

now! Why in the world would you ..."

"You are not my employee Mr. Schaefer, you work for Newburg. You have been briefed. Go back to your ship." Campo said this dismissively, as if Mark's plea was irrelevant. As if Keith's life was irrelevant.

That was a mistake.

"Let Caesar and Reed in. They are probably at the gate right now." As he said this, Mark's cell phone buzzed. The text message read, "We're here!"

"Those men no longer work for St. John's. They will be arrested if they step one foot on this property," Jabber said.

Mark was through talking. Keith might be dying and the other men stuck in there with him were also in peril.

Reaching back, Mark pulled out his silver revolver that he had tucked in his pants and hidden underneath his light jacket. He walked around the desk, cocked the trigger and put the gun to Jabber Campo's head.

"Open the gate, Mr," Mark said.

Terrified, Jabber ordered his men to let Caesar and his entourage through. Mark listened and heard Caesar's voice saying that he was inside.

"Those men are armed, Campo. The people who

work here consider themselves to be a family. If you or your rent a cops make one move to stop us, they will not hesitate to open fire. Neither will I."

As the phone in Campo's office started to buzz, the security guards returned just in time to witness Mark shoving Campo back into his chair.

Still holding the gun Mark said, "Get out of my way."

The guards were not foolish enough to try and stop Mark.

One of the guards then said, "New York is on the line, Mr. Campo. They say it's urgent".

The media had not only filmed the whole scene at the entrance gate, they followed Caesar and Reed onto the Yard. The networks were reporting that the Shipyard CEO, one Mr. Jabber Campo, was delaying rescue efforts, refusing to allow men who could help access to the property.

Jabber punched line one. "Bill, let me explain. I had to ..."

"Stand down, Jabber. I'm coming down there right now on our corporate Leer. For the next few hours anyone who has a question or concern is to call me."

"You're firing me? *Me?*" Jabber was

incredulous.

"You'll be lucky if I don't shoot you and roll you into the harbor. You're only a message taker now, Jabber. Please don't do one more stupid thing or I swear to G..."

Campo slammed down the phone. He couldn't believe it. After decades of loyal service he was just summarily dismissed? Like some loser flunky?

Nineteen

"When's the last time you talked to Keith?" Billy Caesar asked, as they loaded the tanks onto the sled, a reinforced cart used to haul heavy pieces of machinery around the Yard.

"Half an hour ago. I guess I'm afraid to call Randy back, I mean what if ..." Mark didn't want to think about it, all he wanted to do was get the tanks and torches in place and cut open the door.

"Harry, have you got the lift?" Billy asked, speaking into the radio.

"Rolling. Meet you at the wing wall," Harry responded.

"Roger that," Billy acknowledged.

"How can I help?" Mark asked.

"Are there three guys around here who know anything?" Caesar asked.

"Maybe, but three is pushing it."

"Get 'em and meet me at the wing wall. Keep everyone else out of my way. Especially that Campo guy."

"Done."

Mark had procured a small motorcycle from one of the men and was using it to move quickly around the Yard. It only took him a couple of minutes to return to the wing wall.

The press was setting up on the dock across from the *Jackson*. Every move anyone made near the wing wall was now being filmed. As Mark pulled up and turned off his bike, three reporters rushed to him barking questions.

"I don't have time for this," Mark said. Security was finally doing something useful; they were keeping the media off of the *Jackson*.

"What's the plan?" one of the men who were trying to fix the disabled pump asked Mark.

"See that?" Mark said, gesturing to a huge lift arriving at the adjacent dock. "Billy is going to load a cutting torch onto the lift. Then they are going to extend the arm of the lift and set the thing right outside the wing wall hatch. Then I start cutting."

"You any good with a torch?" the man asked.

"I'll do when I'm motivated. Any word from the men trapped inside?"

"Everyone is alive, but your friend... he's not doing well. Randy is doing his best, but ..."

Mark just couldn't bear to think about it. He gathered up all the gear he would need, goggles, welding suit, boots, which had been delivered a few minutes earlier to the Pump Room. Seconds later he heard the high pitched whirr of the lift delivering the welder to the open hatch. Then Billy and Harry climbed in through the hatch.

"We'll set it up, Mark. When we give you the high sign, spark it and start cutting. Ten minutes tops and you'll have a man sized hole," Harry Reed said.

By the time the men finished stretching out the

hoses Harry gave Mark the thumbs up. With a loud pop the welder came to life. Mark knew right where to start, the bottom right corner of the hatch which had been jammed into the frame. That's where the metal would be thinnest.

"What was that?" Billy Caesar asked. A loud thump, that could be felt as well as heard, reverberated through the wing wall.

"Could be anything," Harry offered. "It sounded like a pipe bursting, or some other metal popping due to stress."

"Hey! Can anyone hear me in there! What on earth is going on!" Randy was yelling into his radio, trying to be heard over some roar.

"This is Harry Reed. What's..."

"The water is pouring in! We've got to get the heck out of here! Maybe fifteen feet left of air space and it's filling up fast!"

Mark nodded his head, he'd felt the vibration and heard enough of the radio message.

"Lord," Mark prayed, "let these hands work quickly. Give me strength."

Harry and Billy stayed in constant contact with the men trapped in the tank. Their pleas for rescue grew more frantic as the water rose.

Mark cut through the bottom three hatch hinges first, making a semi-circle. Then he made a decision. He wasn't sure how long Keith had left so he cut straight down each side knowing that the pressure of a wall of water could knock him over. But if the water was rising that was the best plan, as long as he didn't get tossed across the room by a three hundred pound steel door.

"Bring me the scissor jacks," Mark yelled over his shoulder.

With only four hinges to go, Mark could hear the men pounding on the other side of the hatch. Water was pouring through the half inch gap in the steel at the bottom. As he got closer to finishing his cut, his mind was racing ahead as the adrenalin was pumping...

Mark stopped cutting for a moment and ordered, "Put those jacks in place sideways from bulk head to bulk head, twelve inches back". After the third scissor jack was in place, he starting cutting the last four hinges. Before he finished his final cut, the water pressure forced the cut hatch piece out and it slammed into the jacks, narrowly missing Mark's head. God let the jacks hold, Mark silently prayed.

A left arm emerged from the opening with a spider

tattoo on it. Keith's arm.

Mark grabbed Keith's arm in an Indian style grip and pulled him to safety before handing him over to the waiting medics. Keith looked pale and nearly spent.

Half conscious Keith managed to eke out, "Thanks, Mark. Knew you would come. Just knew it." Then he passed out.

A few seconds later Keith's heart stopped beating. The EMTs worked feverishly on him doing their best to keep him alive long enough to get him to the hospital where they could treat his injuries.

They used the same lift that once held the torches to lower Keith down to the waiting ambulance. Mark was with Keith all the way holding his right arm and praying as hard as he could for God to save his best friend.

Twenty

"Mark," Joy yelled. "Telephone."

"Who is it, hon?" Mark asked.

"Billy."

"I'll pick up in the garage," Mark said. He put down the pliers and screwdriver that he was using to fix Fletcher's flat bicycle tire and walked into the garage. Mark picked up the ancient handset they had wired and sitting on his workbench.

"It's official," Billy Caesar said. "Welcome to St. John's Shipyard Mr. Schaefer."

"Really? Did they give me what I asked for?"

"Seventy grand a year, plus benefits. I know it's a pay cut Mark, but we'd be glad to have you if you'll come."

"Reassure me again that Bowman will leave the Yard alone."

"They won't leave us totally alone, Mark. But they will not mess with what works. The union stays, the men stay. The labor contract comes up for renewal in a few months and there will be some givebacks, there has to be, given the economy. The union gets that too. Andy was a generous man; Bowman has a different agenda. But, hey, they gave me a five year contract with stock options as Yard Manager and they hired Harry back too. We will make the Yard a great place to work again, you'll see."

"What about Mike Patty?"

"You didn't hear?" Billy asked.

"Hear what?"

"The day after you rescued those ..."

"We, Billy. We."

"The day after *we* rescued Keith and the men,

Mike went over to Jabber's apartment and beat him up. Laid him out good and proper."

"I wish I could have seen that!"

"That sorta took Mike out of the running for a job with Bowman, but he didn't want one anyway. Jabber was persuaded not to press charges by Langston."

"Where is Mr. Campo? Does anyone know? Or care?"

"Forced early retirement. He no longer works for the company."

"I've been praying for him."

"There you go, doing the right thing again."

Mark laughed. He knew that he would love working for Billy Caesar.

"How's Keith?" Billy asked.

"Still in the hospital. It's been almost two weeks now, but he gets out tomorrow. He'll be staying with us for a while. Joy is going to nurse him back to health."

"You know, Mark, by all rights Keith should be dead. He was bled out inside before he reached the hospital. Like the doctors said on TV, they couldn't figure out how he was still breathing. It was a miracle."

"Is it enough to get you back in the pew?"

"Yea, Mike promised to drag me to Mass."

"We've got a spot in our Church for you too, Billy. Love to have you visit some Sunday."

"You know what, Mark, I just might. Just might."

"See you Monday morning?"

"Bright and early, Schaefer. Work starts at seven."

"Yes sir," Mark said with a smile.

Joy had been watching and listening as she leaned against the entrance to the garage. Tears were flowing down her cheeks. She walked over and gave her husband a huge hug and a long, deep kiss.

"I guess I'm home for good, babe," Mark said. "Hope you won't get sick of having me around all the time."

"Never, Mr. Schaefer. Never."

The End

Published Titles by *Arise Publishing* can be purchased at:
http://www.amazon.com/author/arisepublishing
(You can also rate this book at the above link)

All books are available as
eBooks on Kindle as well as **Paperback**.

Visit us at www.arisepublishing.com
for updates on titles that are
coming soon.

Printed in Great Britain
by Amazon